Targeted

Book nine of the Jenny Watkins Mystery Series

1. Driven
2. Betrayed
3. Shattered
4. Exposed
5. Trapped
6. Vindicated
7. Possessed
8. Haunted

Copyright 2016

Dedication

As always, I have so many people to thank. First, my family deserves recognition for their love and support throughout this whole process. Scott, Hannah, Seneca, Evan and Julia, I couldn't do this without you.

Next, I have to acknowledge the role Lauren Brennan played in this book. She was the winner of my "100th Amazon review" contest, so many of the character names and plot twists are at her request. (More thanks to Mark for cluing me in on some extras.) I only hope the book does her justice.

My proofreaders, once again, are invaluable to me. Danielle Bon Tempo and Bill Demarest, you catch the mistakes I never would. Marla Musatow, thank you for giving me the thumbs up. I cannot express how much your input helps me with this process.

The cover models you see are such good sports. Complete strangers to each other, Cassie Craze agreed to go to Sophie and Mia DeSantis's house so I could take the photo. (I am so happy to know twins who could make this cover happen. ☺)Thank you, ladies, for your willingness to help…especially when your "payment" is free books. LOL

Lastly, thanks to you, my readers, for faithfully following Jenny Larrabee through her journey. I love to write about her, so I'm glad you like to read it ☺

And now, I hope you enjoy Targeted…

Chapter 1

"It's all about expectations," the counselor said.

Dr. Krafts appeared to be in her late fifties; the pictures plastered all over her quaint little office implied she had several grown children of her own. Jenny had faith that she knew what she was talking about, not just as a highly-recommended psychologist, but as a mother who had been through the newborn years herself.

"Expectations?" Jenny asked. Her exhausted brain was having trouble grasping anything that wasn't expressly spelled out for her.

"Yes," Dr. Krafts replied, "expectations. People have a hard time dealing with situations when they anticipate something pleasant but are met with something that isn't. I imagine you thought motherhood would look a lot different than what you are experiencing."

"You got that right," Jenny muttered bitterly. Her filter hadn't worked properly since the birth of her baby a few weeks earlier, and, as a result, her mouth always said anything that popped into her mind.

"That happens a lot," the counselor said matter-of-factly. "Many people—especially women—tend to romanticize what parenthood will be like. People will tell you it's hard, and while you're pregnant, you acknowledge it's going to be hard. But the reality is, you don't know just how hard it is until after the baby is born, and, at that point, you find yourself bewildered."

"Bewildered," Jenny repeated. "Is that the polite term for *wanting to punch everybody in the face?*"

Dr. Krafts let out a laugh. "I used the more technical term." Tucking her hair behind her ear, she added, "Let me ask you this...Did anyone tell you what to expect ahead of time? Do you have any previous experience with newborns? Or did you go into this completely blind?"

Jenny recalled a conversation she'd had with a woman named Kayla, who told her how difficult newborn babies were. "I did have a warning, I guess," she confessed. "But, honestly, at the time, I just thought the woman was being negative. I figured she just didn't want to be a mother as much as I did." Jenny looked down at her lap.

With a reassuring smile, Dr. Krafts said, "It's okay. We all do it. It's funny—we often ask people for advice, but then we disregard any advice that doesn't align with what we are already thinking. I've seen so many cases where women have been told to leave their husband a hundred times over by a hundred different people, but they instead choose to listen to the one person who says, 'Oh, he'll outgrow it. Just give him time.'"

Jenny didn't say anything, silently acknowledging she had been guilty of that. She had been positive that she was going to love motherhood, and she completely dismissed anything that suggested otherwise.

And now, here she was, so desperate to run away from home that she couldn't breathe.

Dr. Krafts uncrossed her legs, leaning forward to put her elbows on her knees. "So, tell me, what did you expect motherhood to be like?"

Blowing out a breath, Jenny thought about the question for a while before answering. "I thought I'd like it, first of all, which I don't." Tears burned the back of her eyes with that statement; admitting the truth made her feel both vulnerable and unworthy. "I thought the baby would be an addition to what I already had going on in my life...like everything would be the same, only better." She closed her eyes and shook her head. "Instead, nothing is the same. I can't eat when I'm hungry or sleep when I'm tired or shower when I feel gross. My entire life has been turned upside-down."

"A baby will do that," Dr. Krafts agreed.

"What gets me the most," Jenny went on, "is that my husband's life has hardly changed at all. He treats parenting like it's optional. I guess, to him, it is. After a couple of minutes of the baby fussing for him, he always just hands him off to me, no matter how fed up I am or how many hours straight I'd been dealing with it."

"Have you told him that you want him to be a more actively involved parent?"

"Repeatedly."

"How have you said it?"

Jenny didn't understand the question. "I've told him, 'You need to be a more actively involved parent.'"

Once again, the counselor laughed. "What I mean is, did you say it when you were in the throes of an emotional moment? Or did you sit down and have a rational conversation with him?"

"Both, I think," Jenny said. "Although, it comes out more when the baby is screaming and I've had it."

"Sadly, that's probably the worst time to bring it up. If you're fed up, the words may come out sounding more like a demand than an expression of your needs. And if you sound like you're being demanding, his natural reaction may be to put his defenses up."

"I understand that," Jenny replied. "I am aware that when I say things, I often sound like I'm nagging. I do remember one particular conversation, though, where we sat down and had a nice discussion about it. He told me that he didn't parent much because he felt like he was bad at it. He said he couldn't ever get the baby to stop crying, but I assured him I couldn't either. I explained to him—very calmly, I might add—that I needed some breaks from the baby, and I asked him to help with that, even if he didn't feel like he was the best father in the world. I thought I'd gotten through to him...that night he actually got out of bed and helped with the baby. But then he went right back to his old ways." At that point, Jenny let out a snort.

"What was that about?" Dr. Krafts asked, referring to the sound Jenny had just made.

Shaking her head and releasing a sigh, Jenny admitted, "He told me that the reason he wasn't helping with the baby more was because I wasn't having enough sex with him."

The counselor remained quiet for a moment before asking, "And what do you think of that statement?"

"I think it's a crock of shit, that's what I think."

Leaning back in her chair, Dr. Krafts seemed to be formulating her words. "Okay," she said calmly, holding up her hand, "I want you to be aware of something."

Jenny braced herself, sensing that this comment was not going to be something she wanted to hear.

"Your husband expressed a need to you with that statement. I understand you may not see the validity of his argument—I mean, with all that you have going on, who cares about sex, right? But to a man, it's different. Sex is very important to them, on a lot of levels. They like the physicality of it, of course, but I think it also makes them feel desirable. If you don't have physical relations with him, it's as if you are rejecting him—and rejection can hurt."

Jenny could feel irritation stirring inside of her. She did not want to be told Zack's point was valid. After working herself to exhaustion since the day the baby was born, was she really being told by a professional that she wasn't doing enough? "So, you're saying I should put out more?" There was more bitterness in her tone than she had wanted.

"I have no idea how much you're putting out," the doctor said with a smile, "so I can't really comment on that. Instead, what I'm saying is, if you want your husband to listen to your needs when you express them, you have to be willing to listen to his. To him, this perceived lack of sex is very real and, apparently, upsetting enough for him to bring up. Whether you agree with it or not is of no consequence. It's what he's feeling, and he expressed it to you. It sounds to me like you dismissed it, much like he dismissed your request to help with the baby—and you know how that felt when he did it to you."

Jenny remained silent.

"It's less about what's being said, and more about being heard," Dr. Krafts went on. "I think neither of you are feeling heard right now, and that's a terrible way to feel."

"I did hear him," Jenny replied, "and I told him I'd have more energy to fool around if he took care of the baby more."

"I understand that," the counselor said compassionately. "Believe me, I do. But what you've said to him, essentially, is that you'll start listening to him only *after* he starts listening to you. It's almost as if you're holding his request hostage."

"I'm not holding it hostage."

"Not intentionally." The doctor's tone was matter-of-fact. "Just like I imagine he's not intentionally hurting you by neglecting his responsibilities as a father. But you two are having a standoff right now, and one of you needs to be the bigger person and compromise first."

"But why does that have to be me? I feel like I've already done way too much compromising." Her previous marriage flashed in her mind, where she was always the one making the concessions. The last thing she wanted to do was get into that situation again.

The doctor shrugged. "It doesn't have to be you. But you came here today because you want things to be different at home, right?"

Once again, Jenny didn't say anything.

"I say this to my clients all the time," Dr. Krafts said softly. "Would you rather be right, or would you rather be happy?"

Letting out a little laugh, Jenny remarked, "Can't I be both?"

"Not always," Dr. Krafts replied with a smile. "But think about it...do you really want to be married to somebody who's always wrong?" After being met with silence, she continued, "Remember, he's not the enemy. He's the person you married, and I assume you married him because you love him."

Jenny responded in a whisper, "I do love him."

"So, my advice is to reach out to him. Offer the olive branch. If you find that you are doing your part and he still refuses to do his, then we can figure out what to do next. But if you honor his requests, there's a chance he will respond in kind. And wouldn't that be great?"

Wouldn't that be great? Jenny asked herself. While the help would have been fantastic, the thought of fooling around with Zack was alarmingly unappealing. She was unsure whether it was hormones or exhaustion that was causing the problem, but she had absolutely no sex drive whatsoever. On top of that, Zack hadn't been all that attractive to her lately. It was hard to feel attracted to him while she was up in the middle of the night—again—and she could hear him snoring from the other room. And he certainly wasn't desirable as he lay on the couch watching television while she dealt with fussing baby all day long.

Truth be told, Jenny didn't feel like Zack deserved sex. It was as simple as that.

"Besides," the doctor continued, breaking Jenny out of her train of thought, "there are worse things in the world than your husband wanting to sleep with you. He still finds you desirable, which is something a lot of married people feel like they can't claim. And remember—sex is supposed to be enjoyable. Perhaps you can even learn to like it again if you stop considering it a bargaining tool."

Jenny cringed internally. When the doctor put it that way, it seemed like a silly thing to be upset over.

"Well," Dr. Krafts added, "our time is just about up. We can schedule another appointment for next week, if you'd like."

Jenny did just that, and then she headed outside on auto-pilot as her brain replayed what had been said during the session. She climbed into the car and turned the key, trying to figure out exactly when sex went from being pleasurable to being a chore that caused her to be resentful. It was the third trimester, she decided, that made the difference. In her second trimester, she couldn't get enough of Zack; when she wasn't with him, she thought about being with him, looking forward to their moments alone together.

It was, essentially, the opposite of how she felt right now.

She imagined what it would have felt like to be in the throes of her second trimester, only to have Zack repeatedly turn her down for sex. He would have been right there in the bed with her, mere inches away and looking very appealing, but refusing to let her touch him. She had to admit that would have been painful, and she imagined after a few months she would have become resentful, too. She probably would have wondered what was so unappealing about her that made Zack not want to be with her. It might have even made her feel detached from him, reluctant to do him any favors considering that he didn't seem to have any regard for her needs.

"How is this happening?" Jenny said out loud as she pulled out of the parking lot. "How am I turning into the bad guy here?"

There is no bad guy, she thought. There was no good guy or bad guy in a healthy marriage. There was no right or wrong. There were only differing opinions and, in this case, misunderstood actions. She drew in a deep breath as she considered the doctor's words. The olive branch needed to be extended, and she could either offer it or wait for Zack to do it. If she waited for Zack, there was a chance they'd be in a stalemate forever.

The reality was, she had married a simple, goofy guy who made her laugh and respected her talents. He had a host of wonderful qualities, but maturity was not necessarily among them. She'd need to be the adult in these situations, whether she wanted to or not. It was part of the price of admission for being married to Zack.

She thought back to Zack's behavior when they'd first met and were nothing more than friends. He was chronically late without apology or warning. He used to show up with food for himself and nothing for her. She told him back then about how important punctuality and consideration were to women, and he really made an effort after that to be more chivalrous.

He had not made a similar effort after the last discussion they'd had about caring for the baby. A small twinge of fear hit Jenny as she drove down the road—perhaps, back in the beginning, he was trying to impress her, and now he wasn't anymore. Maybe he was feeling disconnected from the marriage, possibly with one foot out the door already. The thought scared her, which, ironically, brought her some comfort. She must have still cared if she was upset by the notion of losing him. At times, lately, she was beginning to wonder if she had any feelings left for him at all.

She would need to remember that he wasn't a given. She couldn't take him for granted, or else she might wake up one day and find him packing his bags. Gripping the steering wheel tighter, she made a vow to reach out to him a little more and stop regarding him as the enemy. She had married him because he made her happy and she loved being with him.

She had to get that back.

Jenny walked into the house to find Zack lying on the couch watching television. She closed her eyes before she spoke, knowing the answer she was about to receive. She spoke sweetly nonetheless. "Hey, honey. Where's the baby?"

"He's with your mom," he replied. "I couldn't get him to stop crying, so I brought him downstairs."

Had she heard those words two hours earlier, she would have been consumed with hate and anger. However, she now realized that this marriage was a work in progress, and she needed to be accepting of his shortcomings.

Or, at least, she needed to try.

Placing her purse on the coffee table, she pointed to the spot next to Zack on the sofa. "Can I sneak in there?"

He scooted to the side, allowing Jenny to lie next to him, her head resting on his shoulder. She closed her eyes again, remembering a time when this was her favorite place to be. She sniffed his scent as she listened to the sound of his heart beating. This was her husband. This was the man she loved. This was not the enemy.

"How was counseling?" he asked.

"Good," she replied. "Informative. She taught me that I've been unfair to you." She gently ran her fingers up and down Zack's chest. "And you've been unfair to me. And if we want the marriage to be happy, we both need to be a little bit better to each other."

"How so?" he asked without contempt.

"Well, we each need to be more accommodating. We both have needs that aren't being met. Yours are sexual in nature, so I'm going to start putting in more effort to make sure those needs get satisfied."

"For real?" he asked, lifting his head off the couch. "I like your counselor."

"Not so fast, there, chief. This is a two way street. You're going to have to help with the baby more."

He made a grunting sound, which Jenny interpreted to be displeasure. "I'm not sure how helpful I'll be," he replied. "I mean, you'd still have to get up in the middle of the night with him. I can't feed him."

Jenny had heard this excuse a million times, and it always infuriated her. However, with her new goal of marital harmony in mind, she simply said, "I plan to buy a breast pump so that I can make some bottles in advance. That way you can experience the joy of a midnight feeding." She tapped him on the chest.

"Me?"

"You." Jenny's tone was light. "The way I see it, this breast pump has the ability to fix the place where Mother Nature screwed up. See, I carried the baby. I dealt with the pregnancy. As far as I'm concerned, I should be done now. *You* should have the breasts so you can take over the responsibilities after the baby is born."

"If I had breasts, I would never leave the house," Zack replied. "I would just stay home and fondle myself all day long."

"There's something wrong with you."

"Just being honest. I think Mother Nature actually knew what she was doing when she put the boobs on the women, considering she probably wanted men to be productive members of society."

"Well, if that's the case, then Mother Nature is a man. It's Father Nature. A woman wouldn't do this to all the other females of the world."

"I disagree. I think Mother Nature simply didn't trust the men enough to give them such a big responsibility. She knew that the dads wouldn't hear the baby cry during football season. Kids still need to eat on Sundays, which is why she gave the boobs to you. Besides, I don't think I would have made it through that whole birth thing. That looked rough."

This was the sense of humor that Jenny had fallen in love with. She had since gotten used to his goofy remarks, so she didn't laugh at them as much as she used to. But they were still there, and she needed to remember that.

"It *was* rough," she replied. "All the more reason you should have the breasts. I will head out to the store after this and get myself that pump."

"Will the sales lady demonstrate how to use it? If so, I'll go with you."

"You're such a pig," Jenny said with a smile.

He shrugged under her head. "I'm a guy. *Pig* goes without saying."

She sighed and repositioned herself so that she was on top of him, her lips just inches from his. Studying his face, she remembered feeling enamored with him once upon a time. While the newness had definitely worn off, she did still love him deep down inside, and she ultimately wanted him to be happy. "I'm sorry if I've been neglecting you. I don't mean to, and it has nothing to do with how handsome you are or anything like that. I just haven't felt very...sexy lately. I felt fat and bloated at the end of the pregnancy, and I've been completely exhausted since the baby was born. I know it wasn't fair of me to jump your bones every chance I got in the second trimester, only to turn around and completely shoot you down after that."

Although he didn't say anything, he ran his hands up and down her back. She had to admit, it felt nice.

"So," she continued, looking at him flirtatiously, "are you willing to strike a deal? We should both make more of an effort to meet each other's needs?"

"Let me confer with Little Zack for a minute." He looked up and to the right as if he was having a conversation inside his head. He quickly gave an emphatic nod, stating, "We are both in agreement that it's a good idea."

He pulled Jenny in close and gave her a kiss.

Chapter 2

Four months later, in April...

"It happened again," Zack announced, looking at his laptop.

"What did?" Jenny grinned at little Steve, who emphatically returned the gesture from his high chair. Cereal oozed down his chin and his legs flailed with happiness. Jenny absolutely adored how he smiled with his whole body, her feelings toward the baby having completely turned around since the newborn days. He was the light of her life, and she couldn't have loved him more if she tried.

Zack's tone was solemn. "Another murder at Perdion University."

The joy left Jenny's body in an instant. "What happened this time?"

"Same as last time," he replied. "A female grad student had her throat slit in her bed."

"That's got to be the work of the same person," Jenny announced.

Zack shrugged. "Could be a copycat."

"Do you really think two people would be capable of something like that?"

"I would hope not, but we shouldn't jump to conclusions."

Jenny shook her head, unable to fathom that even one person had that type of violence in him...or her. Like Zack said, she shouldn't jump to conclusions. "Do they have any suspects?"

"They did, until the second incident," Zack said. "According to this, they originally thought the first victim must have known the killer personally. There was no sexual assault, nothing was taken...there weren't even any signs of torture, so it wasn't a pleasure killing. It appeared as if the killer just wanted this particular girl dead, so they were looking at people that may have had a vendetta against her. But now that they've got this second victim killed in a similar fashion, they don't know what to make of it."

"Did the girls know each other?"

"That's what they're investigating. They went to the same school, but it doesn't look like they did."

"Could they have had a mutual acquaintance?"

"Apparently, they had a sick and twisted mutual acquaintance."

Steve fussed, reminding Jenny that she had been forgetting to feed him while she had this conversation. Spooning a bite of cereal into his mouth, she looked at him with a broken heart. She had been freezing her breast milk, saving it for a day when she'd have to leave town to investigate a difficult homicide. This murder spree certainly sounded like it qualified, but the thought of leaving her baby behind with her mother for a few days was nearly unbearable.

Her focus shifted, however, to the two mothers whose babies had just been murdered by a psychopath. Jenny was upset about not seeing her son for a few days—these women were without their children for a lifetime, and there could have been more grieving mothers if this killer wasn't caught.

While she would miss her baby dearly, she knew she had to go and do her part. She reached out and touched Steve's face, fully aware that he would understand this one day considering he had also been born with psychic ability.

"Are you thinking what I'm thinking?" Jenny asked Zack.

He looked up from his laptop. "I'll start packing a bag."

During the drive, Zack had called the Girard County Police Department in Bennett, Missouri, where Perdion University was located. He had informed them that he and Jenny were on their way, sending them links to articles featuring the previous murders that Jenny had helped solve. The woman on the phone had been surprisingly accommodating, putting Zack on hold briefly before telling him that the chief was glad they were coming. She told them they should ask for Detective Savannah Brennan when they arrived, which, after the six hour drive, would be in the early evening.

Once Zack and Jenny reached the station, they walked to the desk, asking the young officer sitting there if they could speak with Detective Brennan. The officer, who literally appeared to be fifteen, sent out some calls on his walkie-talkie, eventually informing them that the detective was on scene, giving them directions to the location. Although getting back in the car was the last thing Jenny wanted to do, she got behind the wheel and started heading to the spot they had been instructed to go.

"Was it just me," Jenny began once she put the car in drive, "or did that kid look like he was in middle school?"

Zack let out a laugh. "Yeah, he did look pretty young."

"How old do you have to be in order to become a cop?" she asked.

With a shrug, he replied, "Twenty-one, I guess?"

Eighteen. After a little math, Jenny realized exactly how much younger that was than her. "Maybe cops still look the same, and I'm just getting old." Her shoulders sunk a little as she drove.

As they made their way down the city streets, Jenny started to notice some academic buildings cropping up among the older homes that lined the roadway. "I guess this isn't a self-contained campus," she noted. "It's just part of the city."

"I like these old houses," Zack said as he looked out the window. "Do you know how nice these were once upon a time?"

While sitting at a red light, Jenny looked at a few of the buildings. They were huge, with columned porches and brick fronts, but there were only about two feet between the buildings. "I bet they've been converted to student apartments."

"And they've been neglected," Zack added. "That's a shame. Although, I guess it wouldn't make sense to put much work into them. A couple of good parties and the place would be trashed anyway."

Jenny felt a slight buzz in her stomach as they approached the house where the latest victim had lived. The physical reaction was good news, leading Jenny to believe that she would be contacted by this young woman. It seemed this long trip wasn't going to turn out to be a waste of time.

The scene was familiar—as with the other crime scenes she'd visited in the past, the house was enveloped in yellow tape, which was in turn surrounded by a mob of reporters and onlookers. While still in the car, Jenny turned to Zack and said, "I'm getting something, which is promising."

"That's good, although you may have a difficult time working your way through that crowd. That's a lot of people in a small space."

She looked beyond him and out the car window, focusing on the people gathered around the tape. Some wore expressions of sadness, some fear, and others bewilderment. Some managed to wear a combination of the three. Jenny shook her head, overcome by the intense emotion emanating from the crowd. Quickly, however, that feeling turned into determination; she wanted to make sure no other crowds had to gather for a similar reason.

Reaching for the door handle, she announced, "I have permission to cross the line, which is a bit surreal, but I think they're willing to try anything to get this case solved. I have to give them credit for being open to using my ability. A lot of departments would have called me a loony."

"It was my fancy talk on the phone that convinced them," Zack replied.

Jenny flashed him a playful look. "And my previous successes had nothing to do with it?"

"Maybe a little, but it was more me."

Without saying another word, Jenny got out of the car and headed toward the mob. She felt strangely important as she worked her way through the crowd, approaching the tape, knowing she would be let through. Once she finally reached the yellow barrier and started to go under, an officer confronted her. "Are you supposed to be here?"

"I am," Jenny explained. "I was asked to meet with Detective Brennan. My name is Jenny Larrabee."

"You the psychic?" he said, louder than Jenny would have wanted.

"Yes, sir."

"Come on back," he said as he lifted the tape. Jenny bowed underneath it, walking toward the house. To Jenny's surprise, flash bulbs started to go off as she crossed the small lawn. She looked toward the cameras with confusion, wondering if she was really photo-worthy. The answer must have been yes; the barrage of bright lights from photographers and news cameras was nearly blinding.

"Pay them no mind," the officer said, placing his hand on Jenny's back and guiding her to the front door, "and try not to touch anything. And here." He handed Jenny a pair of shoe covers. "Put these on before you go inside."

After sliding her feet into the covers, she clasped her hands together in front of her chest, making an extra effort to keep her fingers off of anything important to the investigation. Once she walked into the house and the officer closed the door behind her, the energy of the crowd disappeared, and a funny feeling took over Jenny's belly. It wasn't enough to provide any information at this point, so she didn't mention it, but she felt confident she'd get something useful out of this visit.

A petite woman with blond hair rounded the corner, sticking out her hand. "Savannah Brennan," she said in a commanding voice, which was in contrast to her pleasant face and tiny body. Even though her expression was serious, she had an appeal to her that made her seem approachable.

"Jenny Larrabee. Thanks for having me today."

"Thanks for coming," the detective replied, shaking her head. "Between you and me, this case has us stumped."

"Does that mean you don't have any leads?" Jenny asked.

"We don't know what we have, other than two dead co-eds," she replied. "How familiar are you with the cases?"

"I only know what I've read, and I'm not sure how much of that is reliable."

"On the Internet? Oh, boy," Detective Brennan said with a roll of her eyes. "Let me tell you the *real* story." Scratching her head, she began, "It all started three weeks ago with our first victim, Song Yi Lee, who goes by Sonya. Twenty-three, Asian, lived alone in a first-floor apartment on Queen Street. She was a grad student at Perdion, studying social work. No known enemies to speak of. She was last seen by her friend, Becca Newman, on Monday evening three weeks ago, when they ran into each other at the grocery store. She engaged in a few text conversations with friends until 10:37 that night, not saying anything unusual. She claimed to be at home studying while those exchanges happened, which her cell phone records verified.

"On Tuesday, she failed to show up for class. Her friends tried calling and texting, but she didn't respond. After a while, the messages went straight to voicemail, presumably because the phone ran out of charge. Concerned, her friend, Maggie Wallace, went over to check on her. When Sonya didn't answer the door, Maggie walked around the perimeter and found the bedroom window open with the screen cut. She immediately called the police, who went in and found Sonya in her bed with a blunt force trauma injury to her head and her throat slit. Based on the position of the body, it appeared she hadn't even woken up before the attack happened."

Jenny curled her lip. "It sounds like the killer was on a mission."

Detective Brennan widened her eyes and nodded emphatically. "There were no signs of the typical motives. No sexual assault. Nothing taken. Nothing ransacked. She wasn't bound or tortured in any way. The perp just clearly wanted her dead for some reason. We had every reason to believe it was personal, so the first place we looked was her romantic history. Nothing says 'you shouldn't have left me' like a quick slit of the throat, right?" She shook her head. "We looked into her dating life, but we weren't able to come up with anyone who stood out as either jaded enough—or crazy enough—to do something that drastic. And then this happened." She swept her arm to the side, gesturing to the apartment on Jenny's right.

"What went on here?" Jenny asked.

"More of the same," Detective Brennan replied. "This victim is Lisa Penne, twenty-two, also a grad student at Perdion, but studying pharmacology. Killed the same way. Also appeared to have been murdered in her sleep. No signs of struggle, no defensive wounds. She was lying on her side in what appeared to be a comfortable position. Nothing in the room was disturbed. Once again, the perp appeared to go in and out of a bedroom window." She looked up at Jenny. "He's like the wind, this one."

"I wonder what his motive is," Jenny said, dumbfounded.

Detective Brennan shook her head. "We don't know, at this point. We can only assume it's personal, but there doesn't appear to be any immediate link between the two victims. The only things they have in common are that they are grad students at Perdion and they lived alone in first-floor apartments. Their fields of study are different enough that they wouldn't have had any of the same classes. According to the officials at Perdion, social work and pharmacology aren't even in the same building. The girls lived on opposite sides of the school, a total of eight blocks apart. They don't have overlapping friends that we are aware of." The detective shrugged her shoulders. "But we are still looking into that. So far, though, we have nothing to suggest they hung around in the same social circles."

"I guess that's where I come in," Jenny said.

"We don't normally rely on psychics, but we usually have a little more to go on than we do this time." Detective Brennan started walking into the apartment, with Jenny following suit. "When you called, the chief seemed grateful. We need *something* to kick start this investigation."

After taking only three steps into the apartment, Jenny announced, "She has a cat."

Detective Brennan looked at her strangely.

"That's not a psychic reading," Jenny clarified. "That's allergies speaking." Her throat was becoming scratchy and her lungs tight. This would have to be a quick visit.

"Will you be okay?"

Jenny nodded. "For a little while. If I stay too long, I'll regret it."

"Well, the attack happened in the bedroom, obviously," Detective Brennan said. "We can lead you there, but don't disturb anything."

"I got that memo already." Jenny walked to the doorway of the bedroom, feeling a large sense of nothing. It wasn't the typical sensation of when she wasn't getting a reading; this seemed more deliberate. Jenny nodded and headed back out toward the front door where she could breathe better.

Detective Brennan was right behind her. "That was fast. Did you get any insight?"

"Of sorts," Jenny said, looking at the hopeful detective. "It seems Lisa doesn't know who did it, either."

Chapter 3

"You mean, a stranger did it?" Detective Brennan asked.

Jenny shook her head. "Not necessarily. When I say she doesn't know who did it, I mean she has no idea if it was her best friend or someone she'd never met. She simply doesn't know who it was."

"Oh, dear," Detective Brennan said. "Does this mean you won't be able to help us?"

"I may not get much from this scene," Jenny replied, "but if I can get into Sonya Lee's apartment, I might be able to get something there."

Jenny froze for a moment, allowing herself to absorb the wave that came over her. Once the image exited her head, she asked, "Is there a walking trail around here? Or a park or something? Something with paths and trees?"

"Buford Park isn't that far," the detective noted. "It has walking trails."

"I may want to check that out," Jenny replied. "I just got a visual of a man sitting on a bench along a paved path. I can't get a good look at his face, but I get the feeling that Lisa had been freaked out by him at one point."

The detective quickly asked, "Does he appear to be older? Younger? Caucasian? African American?"

Closing her eyes to recapture the image, Jenny said, "Older. Graying hair. Caucasian. He's looking down in the vision I have, so I can't get a good look at his face. He appears a little dirty and unkempt, though, like he could be homeless. Maybe that was what made Lisa uncomfortable?"

Detective Brennan nodded but didn't write anything down, causing Jenny to realize that she hadn't said anything meaningful.

As the cat dander began to catch up with her in the hall, Jenny asked, "Is there any way I can take a look at the other crime scene? I'm hoping I can get a little something more there."

"I think that can be arranged," the detective said. "That apartment is not considered a crime scene anymore, and I believe it's still vacant. Go figure, nobody wants to rent that place after what happened."

"I can't imagine why," Jenny replied dryly.

"Let me get on the phone with the landlord; I'll tell him to let you in. He shouldn't argue—he wants this thing solved as much as anybody. Besides, he's a twitchy little guy. I'm pretty sure he'd do anything we told him to."

"How many apartments are in that building?" Jenny asked.

"Four," Detective Brennan said as she pulled out her phone, "but everyone has moved out except for one person."

"Hmmph," Jenny grunted.

"I know." The detective pushed some buttons on her phone, placing it to her ear. "Suspicious, right? He was on the suspect list, believe me. You should see the guy…he's got to be six-nine or…Hello, Mr. Hallberg?" She interrupted herself, speaking into the phone. "Detective Brennan. I have a woman here who would like to get into Sonya Lee's apartment to do some investigating. I was hoping you'd be able to let her in."

Jenny waited in silence as the detective listened.

"Great. Thanks," Detective Brennan said. "She can be there in about five minutes, I'm guessing. Her name is Jenny Larrabee." She hung up the phone and, without missing a beat, added, "Six-ten. He's the center for the basketball team."

"Is he skinny enough to fit through a window?" Jenny asked.

"Absolutely. He looks like he was once a normal-sized guy who was put on a rack and stretched out. But we haven't discounted that the slit screen may have been a ruse, designed to throw us off. It could be that it was an inside job, and the killer got in some other way. Shit, for all we know, he could have been invited in. That doesn't bode well for the neighbor...he claims that he and Sonya were friendly."

"They were friendly?" Jenny repeated. "Not friends, but *friendly*?"

"I asked him about that, too. It was a strange way to put it. He said he didn't mean it in a sexual sense; they were just acquaintances. Although, that doesn't mean he didn't want it to be sexual." She looked at Jenny with raised eyebrows. "That could provide a nice little motive, couldn't it? Although, it wouldn't explain a damn thing about what he would have been doing over here, or how he got in." She pointed toward Lisa's apartment. "Why don't you get on over there and see what you can find. God knows we're not figuring a whole lot out the old fashioned way."

"Will do. But first, can you tell me the name of the basketball player and exactly which apartment he lives in?"

"His name is Luke Thomas, and he lives directly upstairs from Sonya." She gave Jenny the address and a brief description of how to get there before ending their meeting with a handshake.

Relieved to be back outside and away from the dander, Jenny headed back to the car and got into the driver's seat, closing the door behind her.

"How'd it go?" Zack asked.

"Lisa Penne—that's her name—didn't know who her killer was. She was sound asleep, apparently, when she got knocked out and her throat got slit. She never saw it coming."

"That's both good and bad, I guess. It was quick, at least."

"If you've got to go so horribly, I suppose quick is best." Jenny stifled a shudder. "But, for my purposes, it would have been better if she could have gotten a look at the guy. My job would certainly be made a whole lot easier." She typed Sonya's address into her phone, allowing the GPS to squawk directions at her. Within two minutes, she and Zack were pulling up to the house in question, getting out of the car into the increasingly dark night. Like Lisa's apartment, Sonya's place appeared to be a large house converted into separate living spaces. There were two doors in the front, next to each other; she imagined each led to two of the four apartments.

Another car pulled up, and a middle aged man emerged. "Hello," he said as he fumbled with a ring full of keys. "Are you Ms. Larrabee?"

"Yes, sir. I'm Jenny, and this is my husband, Zack."

He bowed several times and waved awkwardly; Detective Brennan's description of *twitchy* was a pretty good assessment.

"Well, let me get you in," the landlord said. "It's terrible what happened, isn't it? I can't help but feel responsible. I should have put bars on the windows. Then the guy could have never gotten in. But, then, imagine if there was a fire; she wouldn't have been able to get out. That definitely would have been a fire hazard. The marshal never would have allowed that." As he spoke, his jittery hands were barely capable of grasping the correct key. Eventually, he opened the front door on the right, which led to both an immediate door and a flight of stairs to the second floor—where Luke Thomas lived. It appeared he walked past Sonya's door every time he left home. While that didn't necessarily make him guilty, it certainly gave him the opportunity to do something horrible with minimal effort and no witnesses.

A second key was used to open Sonya's door. Jenny acknowledged there were safety measures in place, which must have given the poor girl a false sense of security. Shaking her head clear of that thought, Jenny walked into the empty apartment, which was initially dark until the landlord turned the overhead light on. The emptiness lasted only a second before Jenny saw the apartment the way it had looked when it was occupied. A red couch was flanked by small, glass top tables. An old tube television sat on an entertainment center in the corner. The coffee table, which was covered in books and papers, was made of wood. The room looked like it had been furnished by yard sales, which Jenny imagined was also true of every other living room near campus.

Almost as soon as the furnishings appeared, they fizzled from view. Jenny looked up at Zack and said, "She's still here."

The landlord looked confused, but Jenny ignored it.

Another vision hit Jenny very quickly, as if Sonya was eager to tell her story. She saw a small, feminine hand wearing bright green nail polish reach out and twist the deadbolt handle and then turn the little lock on the door knob itself.

After the brief vision, she announced, "The cut screen wasn't a ruse. She had locked the doors. The guy definitely came in through the window."

"Or he had a key," Zack said.

With those words, the already-nervous landlord looked as if he could have passed out. He opened his mouth to speak, but only a squeaky sound came out.

"A key wouldn't have undone the deadbolt," Jenny replied, holding up her hand in the landlord's direction. "Don't worry, sir, you're off the hook."

He relaxed to the point of becoming physically shorter.

"I don't think I told you," Jenny continued to Zack, "but there's a guy upstairs who is tall enough to take on any woman, from the sound of it. And he's the only one who didn't move out after the incident, is that correct?" She turned her attention back to the landlord.

"That's right. He said he wasn't worried about intruders. In fact, he said he hoped the guy would come back so he could get revenge for Ms. Lee."

"How about the tenants that left?" Jenny asked. "Were they male or female?"

"Both female."

Jenny cocked her head to the side as she processed the information. It made sense; no woman would want to live in that complex after that kind of attack. An athletic man wouldn't have been as afraid.

"Do you mind if I go into the bedroom?" Jenny asked.

"Go right ahead," he said. "I'll just wait out here, if it's all the same to you."

Somehow, Jenny wasn't surprised by that response. She and Zack walked alone into the only bedroom, where she paused to try to get a feel for what the room could tell her. As was the case in Lisa's apartment, she got the impression that the victim had no idea who the killer had been. Sonya had gone straight from sleeping to dead with no period of awareness in between.

Jenny hung her head with defeat. "I've got nothing," she admitted. "We're going to have to go about this a different way. The victims don't even know who we're dealing with."

"What are we going to do, then?"

She let out a sigh and put her hands on her hips. "I guess we'll have to try to find out what places the victims had been—see if there were any links between the two. Maybe I can go to those places and get some insight that the police can't? I don't know."

Zack wordlessly put his arm around Jenny's shoulder.

"At Lisa's place, I got a vision of a guy sitting on a bench by a walking trail. He definitely creeped her out; I guess I can start by looking into that." She glanced up at Zack. "Although, I have to admit, he didn't look all that scary to me. He appeared to be homeless, which may have made Lisa uncomfortable, but you and I both know that homeless doesn't mean violent." She thought back to her last case, where she helped a Veteran with PTSD who had been living on the streets.

For a brief moment, she wondered how he was doing.

"You have to trust your Spidey-senses, though," Zack replied, snapping Jenny out of her thoughts. "Homeless doesn't mean violent, but if Lisa was creeped out by the guy, there may have been a reason for it."

Jenny nodded, silently agreeing to his statement. "I also want to talk to Luke Thomas, the guy upstairs. I have this visual in my head that the guy looks like Plastic Man and could worm his way through any window he wanted."

"Where is that coming from?" Zack asked.

Jenny laughed. "He's been described as extremely tall and skinny. Detective Brennan said he looks like he's been stretched out on a rack. He's on the suspect list in this case, simply because he lives upstairs, but it sounds like he has the build that would allow him to sneak in through windows if he wanted."

"Do you think he's home?"

With a shrug of her shoulder, Jenny replied, "There's only one way to find out."

The couple walked back out into the living room where the landlord nervously played with his fingers. "Did you get everything you needed?"

Jenny smiled graciously. "Yes, sir. From here, anyway. I'd like the chance to talk to the upstairs tenant if he's around, but you don't need to be here for that."

With a move that was a combination of a bow and a nod, the landlord said, "Well, I'll just lock up here, I guess."

The couple walked past him, waiting in the narrow entryway while he made sure the door was secure. They thanked him for his time, heading up the stairs while the landlord went outside.

The stairs did a switchback halfway up, leading to a door that was in the same location as Sonya's but on the second floor. Jenny knocked, hearing commotion come from behind the door. Eventually, she heard an alarmingly deep voice say, "Yeah?"

"Hi, Mr. Thomas. My name is Jenny Larrabee; I'd like to speak to you about Sonya Lee, if you're willing."

She heard some clicking as the locks became undone. The door opened to reveal one of the tallest men she'd ever seen in her life. He had black hair and soft brown eyes with long lashes, making him look like a harmless person, despite his towering presence. "Hey," he said, "come on in."

They stepped inside the apartment, which had the exact same layout as Sonya's. "Thanks for seeing us," Jenny began. "This is my husband Zack; we're trying to get some answers on behalf of Sonya Lee and Lisa Penne. Is it okay if we ask you some questions?"

He nodded his head and looked down, sadness apparent on his face. Gesturing toward his sofa, he said, "You can sit down if you want. I know the routine by now. You're, like, the millionth people to come here and ask me about it."

"Thanks. I'll try to be quick; I don't want to bother you," Jenny replied as she and Zack both took him up on his offer to sit down. Once she was comfortable on the couch, a quick wave hit Jenny, leading her to point to the other side of the room. "The sofa used to be over there, no?"

Luke flashed her a confused look as he sat in the recliner, making the chair look like a miniature. "Yeah. How do you know that?"

Zack chimed in, "She's a psychic, believe it or not."

Looking back and forth between Zack and Jenny, Luke simply said, "What?"

Jenny smiled modestly. "He's right. That's why I'm here. I'm hoping I can get a little insight that the regular police detectives can't get. I'm under the impression that Sonya has been here before, but the furniture looked different." She closed her eyes, recalling the brief image that had flashed into her mind. With each statement accompanied by a point, she added, "The sofa was there, the recliner was there, and the television was along that wall."

"That's right," Luke said with awe. "I rearranged right after Sonya was…attacked. I put shit in front of the windows so that if anyone tried to sneak in, they would knock something over and I would hear them."

Jenny looked around at the arrangement, noticing the shelving units blocking the windows, deeming that his story had merit.

"And then," Luke added, "I'd grab one of the bats I have lying around, and I would clobber the shit out of the guy." He gestured toward them with his head. "Go ahead. Look under the couch."

Zack bent forward and lifted the skirt at the bottom of the sofa. "Yup," he confirmed. "There's a bat there."

"Damn straight there's a bat there. If this guy comes back, he's all mine. After all, who would you put your money on? Some coward with a knife, or a giant pissed-off guy with a bat?"

Jenny felt a warmth encompass her body; Sonya was clearly pleased by this conversation. Jenny imagined that the two neighbors had a good relationship.

"My money's on you, big guy," Zack said emphatically. "I wouldn't want to be on the receiving end of one of your swings."

"Unfortunately, I don't think it will ever happen," Luke added. "It seems this asshole only likes to attack women—when they're sleeping, no less, and have no chance to defend themselves." Luke leaned back in the chair, stretching his legs out in front of him, crossing them at the ankles.

Jenny couldn't help but feel like this was not the demeanor of a murderer who was being questioned about the attack.

"What type of relationship did you have with Sonya?" Jenny asked.

"We were friendly," he said, repeating Detective Brennan's words.

Jenny still found the phrasing to be odd. "You were friends?"

He squinted and tilted his head to the side. "*Friends* might be too strong of a word. We never hung out or anything, but we would stop and talk if we ran into each other. She was a nice person."

Jenny was confused. "But she'd been in your apartment..."

"Yeah," he replied. "She locked herself out once, and she hung out up here until the locksmith came, but that was it."

The term suddenly made more sense to Jenny, who no longer believed that *friendly* was meant to have sexual overtones. "She called you *Shorty*." The words popped out of Jenny's mouth before she even realized what she was saying.

Luke studied Jenny with a mixture of awe and skepticism for a moment, before admitting, "Yeah, that's right. She was, what, five-two or five-three?" A nostalgic smile crept onto his lips when he added, "I called her *Boss*."

There was little doubt in Jenny's mind that she was talking to an innocent man. "I imagine you've already told the police this, but did you hear anything that night?"

Luke sounded bitter. "From what I understand, there wasn't anything to hear. Besides, if I did hear anything, I would have gone down to help her."

"Did you know Lisa Penne at all?"

"The second victim?" Luke asked. "No, I didn't know her."

Jenny nodded, feeling like they weren't going to get any more information out of this man, who just happened to live near the first victim. Standing up, she said, "Well, I don't want to take up any more of your time. I just wanted to get a feel for the dynamic in this apartment building."

"It was a great place to live until a few weeks ago. Now I'm the only one here." Luke also stood up to walk them out.

Jenny looked at him compassionately. "Well, hopefully they'll catch this guy soon, and everybody can move back in."

"Do me a favor, if you can," Luke said. "If you are the one to figure out who this guy is, tell me before you tell the police. I'll go visit him with my bat and let him know what I think of him."

Jenny smiled and extended her hand. "It's a great offer, but I make no guarantees."

Luke grasped Jenny's hand into his, and another surge of warmth ran through her body. This was a good man standing in front of her.

They would need to look elsewhere for the killer.

Chapter 4

"I'm so conflicted," Jenny admitted as they settled into the hotel room. "It's my first night away from the baby, and I feel like I should be there with him. I miss him. But, at the same time, I'm looking forward to a solid night of sleep where I don't have to listen for him." She looked at Zack with helplessness. "And that makes me feel guilty."

"I swear, I don't know why you do this to yourself. You're here, so you might as well just enjoy it."

"But what if my mother is overwhelmed? What if the baby isn't happy with her?"

"It's his grandma; she's going to spoil the crap out of him. Besides, he sees her every day. It's not like you left him with a stranger."

"But what if my mom can't handle it?"

"She's had four kids; I think she can handle it. And you have to admit, five-month-old Steve is a lot easier to deal with than newborn Steve. She'll be fine."

Although she didn't argue, Jenny stuck her lip out in a pout.

"You know what I think?" Zack began as he approached her, wrapping his arms around her waist.

She knew what was coming.

"I think we should take advantage of our time alone and have a little grown up fun."

"I'm so surprised to hear you say that," she replied dryly.

"Well, it's our first night alone in months. We can even get a little loud if we want." His smile was wide and toothy.

While Jenny wasn't necessarily in the mood, the man had a point. "Okay, just let me pump a bottle first."

"That's so not sexy," Zack said.

With a laugh, she replied, "I can't help it. I am used to the baby eating every few hours. I'm getting backlogged. I don't think it would be a good idea for you to start playing around with these things until I take care of business."

He held up his hands. "I don't think I really want to know the details. Why don't you just do what you've got to do, and let me know when you are done?"

Since the machine was loud, Jenny went into the bathroom to do the pumping. She had to admit there was a good deal of relief that came with it; she hadn't done anything resembling nursing in far too long. The down side, however, was that she was now committed to the machine for the next few minutes. She sat on the closed toilet lid and allowed her mind to wander.

So far, the only clue she had from either of the girls was the disheveled man along the walking trail. Closing her eyes, she envisioned him once again, wondering what led him to his apparent homelessness. Had it been drugs? Alcohol? Mental illness? She shook her head, acknowledging that something, somewhere, had gone terribly wrong for that man. The notion saddened her.

She thought back to Mick, who became homeless when his alcohol problem had gotten to be too much. She didn't blame him for drinking so heavily, though, when she considered that he was only trying to erase the horrible images that haunted him from his time in the war. It didn't seem right to her that a man who had fought for his country came home and was essentially forgotten. She wondered if something similar had happened to the man who frightened Lisa in the park. She grew even sadder.

Glancing down at the bottles, she noted they were only partly full. Still glued to the machine, she thought about John for a moment, wondering if he was still in control of his crack addiction. He had never been homeless, but he paid his rent with drug money. He had a sad story to share as well, having lost both his parents—and, consequently, everything else—at a young age. Shaking her head, she realized that many people who were looked down upon were mere victims of bad luck. They deserved a little more understanding and a little less judgment.

And maybe some help.

This train of thought led her to realize how long it had been since she'd checked in with Mick and John. The roommates were supposed to be keeping each other clean, and she assumed that no news was good news, but she made a mental note to contact them shortly. The last thing she wanted was to fail as their support network.

Switching gears, she began to wonder what the best plan of attack would be in the morning. She wanted to go to the walking trails, certainly, to look for this man; that was the only clue she had at this point. Although, she wondered if Sonya ever used those trails. Lisa was the only one to give her that clue. Perhaps that was going to be a waste of time.

Jenny acknowledged this was going to be an especially difficult case. If the girls themselves didn't know who killed them, the best they could do was guess, leading Jenny to places where they may have encountered the perpetrator while they were alive. This could have been a time consuming process that led nowhere.

She wondered if the two victims were aware of each other in the spirit world. Lisa had undoubtedly heard about Sonya before she died, but was she able to seek out Sonya's spirit afterward? Could they confer, comparing notes, figuring out with certainty the things the police could only guess about? Was Sonya aware of Lisa's suspicions about that man in the park? Had she actually seen the same man but experienced less concern? Or were they each flying solo, both still completely mystified about what had happened to them and why?

It was not lost on Jenny that these crimes could have been completely random, and no amount of research of the girls' whereabouts before the murders would lead to any conclusions. Some sick person may have just looked into their windows, realizing they lived alone, and could have chosen his targets that way.

However, if the person had been doing this for some kind of thrill, she imagined there would have been a more ritualistic nature to the killings. For whatever reason, it seemed the perpetrator wanted these women dead. No fanfare. No satisfaction. Just results.

What was it about these women that made them targets? Jenny released a sigh as she realized she had no idea.

She glanced down at the full bottles, unhooking herself from the machine and dumping the contents down the sink. She cleaned everything up and brushed her teeth, well aware of the task that lay ahead of her. Once she finished up in the bathroom, she walked around the corner, taking a look at her husband, who was watching television on the bed. "Hey, baby," she said with a smirk, placing one hand against the wall and the other on her hip. "Come here often?"

"You're a celebrity," Zack announced in the morning, looking at his laptop.

"How so?" Jenny ran a comb through her wet hair.

"Look. You're an Internet sensation."

She walked over to him, peering over his shoulder. She saw a picture of herself walking toward Lisa Penne's house, with a headline that read, "Stumped Police Department Calls in Tennessee Psychic."

"What the hell?" Jenny asked, standing back up. "Why am I news?"

"The article is focusing on how unproductive and incompetent the Girard County police department is."

Faking a smile, Jenny simply said, "Great. And the fact that this guy leaves no clues has nothing to do with it, right?"

Zack shrugged. "I didn't write it. I'm just telling you what it says."

Jenny walked away with disgust, putting the comb back down on the dresser. Her phone chirped; after reading the screen, she announced, "It's a text from Detective Brennan. She says they're having a meeting at the police station at ten o'clock this morning and the chief wants me to attend." She looked over at Zack with an expression of surprise. "Wow. It's a little bit strange that they want me there, don't you think? At the *police* meeting?"

"Not necessarily. If they want you on their team, it makes sense that they'd like you to be in the know. Besides, you can give them information that no one else can."

"I've just never been so involved before," Jenny replied. "I've always been an outsider, maybe working with one officer, and usually on the sly. Or I have investigated completely on my own."

Zack saluted her from his chair. "Welcome to the big leagues, kid."

Jenny continued to squint as she contemplated the situation some more. "I wonder why this chief is so receptive to me. Do you think he's desperate?"

With a laugh, Zack replied, "You really don't think very highly of yourself, do you? Maybe he's just a believer."

"Either way," Jenny said as she began to sort through her suitcase, "I need to get going. I don't want to be late for this thing. It's a miracle I was even invited."

"Go get 'em, tiger," Zack said to her. "Show 'em how it's done."

Jenny wasn't sure how the press knew about this meeting, but they were standing in droves outside of the police station. Puffing out a quick breath for strength, she hopped out of the car, hoping she could remain inconspicuous.

She didn't.

The reporters even knew her name, shouting at her to answer their questions as she approached the front door. The clicks of the cameras echoed in her ears as she kept her gaze forward and her face expressionless. She made it to the double glass doors, grateful for the silence once they closed behind her.

"Hi," she said to the officer behind the desk, "I'm here for the meeting. My name is Jenny Larrabee."

After checking her license, the officer led her back to a conference room that had a white board on wheels on one end of the room and a long table surrounded by chairs. About a dozen detectives of different ages, genders and races were in various places throughout the room, but they all had one thing in common—coffee. Every last one of them held a cup in their hands, which Jenny determined was to make up for the sleep they had undoubtedly been lacking since the attack on Sonya Lee three weeks before.

Detective Brennan came over to her, greeting her with a smile. "Jenny...glad you could make it. Want a cup of coffee?"

Just as Jenny was about to decline, a realization hit. For the first time in over a year, she was neither pregnant nor nursing. She actually *could* have coffee—with caffeine—that magical boost she'd been missing so desperately for the longest time. "That would be fabulous," she replied, eagerly heading to the coffee maker in the corner of the room before taking a seat near the end of the table.

Once everyone was situated, the man Jenny assumed to be the chief started speaking. He was middle-aged and balding, his sunken eyes indicating he was running on less sleep than anyone else in the room. "Okay, everyone, we've got another long day in front of us. Let's go ahead and get started so we can get out of here and get this guy off the streets, shall we?"

Jenny's eyes circulated the room. Some of the detectives ignored her, others seemed curious about her presence. She felt awkward as the chief announced, "We do have a visitor with us today. This is Jenny Larrabee; she's a psychic. I know some of you may not believe in that, but I want you to respect her anyway. We need all the help we can get in this case."

With that, all of the curious eyes left her and focused on the chief.

"Okay, what we have are two dead women, with the same M.O...entry through a window, a quick and dirty execution and an exit out the same window. He doesn't seem to spend much time at the scene, limiting the amount of evidence he leaves behind. We did find a shoe print in the mud outside the window at Lisa Penne's house...size fourteen running shoe, so we're either dealing with a big guy or a little guy who wore big shoes to throw us off.

"We also found black fibers on the window sill of the Penne scene, but that doesn't tell us a whole lot. It was a nighttime attack. The guy dressed for the occasion, which only means he would be harder for potential witnesses to spot.

"The women were facing opposite directions in their beds, so it appears the perp used his left hand on one woman and his right on the other. The slits were both down to up, so he started low and went high.

The medical examiner thinks he knocked them out with a swift blow to the head first, then slit their throats. Both were very quick, intentional acts.

"Blood droplets led to the windows in both cases, indicating a point of exit, although no weapon has been found. The blood all belonged to our victims; he apparently didn't cut himself in the process. No foreign fingerprints were found at either scene, an indication he wore gloves." The chief wiped his hand across his forehead, looking both exhausted and overwhelmed. Without looking at the person in question, he simply asked, "Hughes, what've you got?"

A man sitting at the table spoke from notes. "Penne had a full load this semester." He listed the times and locations of all of her classes. "Went to the university gym at least five times a week, usually in the mid-morning. Was a jogger; liked to run at Buford Park. Hung out in the usual places on Center Street—Shenanigans, Eddie's Brewery and the Tap House, in that order. Worked part time as a waitress at the Athens Diner. Wasn't in a relationship at the time of the murder. Had no bitter ex-boyfriends to speak of. Got a list of names of the men she had been romantically involved with recently; none of them overlap with the Lee case."

The chief had written the important points on the whiteboard in quick, sloppy handwriting. Replacing the cap on the marker, he noted, "It looks like the areas of overlap are the gym, Buford Park and the bars." He closed his eyes. "Who had gym?"

"Me, sir," a woman stated, referring to the sheet in front of her. "Over five hundred students belong to that gym, so it's obviously difficult to get a feel for everyone who's there. I've been focusing on the times that Sonya Lee worked out, which was usually early evening. A few members had told me of a particularly odd student who seemed to be spending more time watching the women than actually working out. His name is Tim Dauber..."

"We're not necessarily dealing with an odd person, here," a man interjected, clearly displeasing the woman who had been speaking. "History suggests this perp would be a fully functioning member of society, not a socially awkward loner. The nature of these attacks makes it seem mission oriented, so I think we need to be focusing on what these women had in common that might have upset this guy. Were they lesbians?

Engaged in interracial relationships? Did they have loose morals? That kind of thing."

The woman directed her comment at the chief. "We can't eliminate the possibility that what these women had in common was that *they were women*. I agree these are most likely mission killings, but we still could be dealing with a socially awkward man who is tired of rejection. Perhaps he found himself attracted to these women, or they both had rejected his advances, and that's what made him feel like they needed to be eliminated."

"This is a college with eight thousand men," another detective stated. "Chances are one of them had unsuccessfully hit on both Sonya and Lisa, especially if both girls worked out at the same gym and hung out in the same bars."

The chief looked at the woman. "Had any men been seen interacting with Sonya at the gym prior to her death? Men that she wasn't necessarily friends with, who may have been hitting on her?"

"No," she replied, "which is why I focused on Tim Dauber; he's the closest thing to a potential suitor I could find there."

The chief closed his eyes, placing his hand on his forehead. "Who had Tap House?"

An older gentleman spoke. "I did. What you have there is three-hundred-fifty drunken college students running around on any given night. It's a whole room full of suspects."

"Anyone stand out?" the chief asked.

"Not that I've been able to determine."

Detective Hughes, who was in charge of researching Lisa, said, "That wasn't Lisa's favorite hang-out. According to her friends, she went there rarely. She much preferred Shenanigans and Eddie's Brewery."

"Shenanigans," the chief said, "go." Jenny could practically see his blood pressure rise with each spoken word.

A woman read from some notes. "Both girls had been known to frequent there; they were considered regulars by the staff. Nothing in particular stood out about these girls prior to their attacks. Nothing suspicious. No one harassing them. There is one man who shows up alone there most nights—a man by the name of Justin Crowling. Mid-forties. Caucasian. Sits at the bar and just watches people."

The same man who interrupted before did it again, placing his head in his hands. "The killer didn't have to be creepy. He could have just talked to them. He could have just given them a smile that wasn't returned, for God's sake. Maybe he just saw them from afar and they triggered something in him." He looked up, repeatedly stabbing his pointer finger into the table for emphasis. "Statistics show the killer is probably an ordinary guy...someone you could talk to and have no idea you were having a conversation with a killer. We are wasting too much time focusing on people who *look* like killers. We need to find the person who *is* the killer. "

The woman's tone escalated. "Yes, but how the hell are we supposed to figure out which men *smiled* at both girls?"

"I can do that," Jenny said softly.

The room instantly became silent; Jenny could feel every eye on her. Clearing her throat, she added, "I can see little snippets of what the girls saw while they were alive." She looked down at the table. "It's how my gift works."

The silence remained, making Jenny want to bolt for the door. After a moment, the chief asked, "Have you seen anything?"

Jenny shook her head. "Only a view of a man in a park, sitting along a jogging trail. He appeared to be homeless. But I might be able to get something else if I went to the other places the victims had been."

The chief looked at her intensely. "Are you willing to go to all of those places?"

"Absolutely."

"Good. Who had Buford?" the chief demanded.

"I did, sir."

"What've you got?"

"Like she said," the man replied, pointing at Jenny, "there is a homeless man who frequents the area. Most of the regulars at the park are familiar with him and say he has always been harmless."

"Look into him. See what he's capable of," the chief demanded. "Who had Eddie's Brewery?"

A man gave a report that sounded similar to the other locations—a million suspects, yet none stood out as particularly promising.

"What about Luke Thomas? Who had him?"

Jenny felt her stomach flutter at the mention of his name. She hoped they would find a piece of evidence that would allow them cross him off the suspect list. She just knew in her heart he didn't do it.

"I did," a man said as he adjusted his tie.

"Any link to Lisa Penne?"

"Basketball practice happened every morning from ten to one. That would have put him at the gym at the same time as Lisa. He's also been known to frequent Shenanigans; it's one of his favorite hang outs."

"Him and half the kids on campus," someone noted.

"At six-foot-ten, he'd have the ability to easily climb in and out of the window," a woman added.

The chief gestured his head in the direction of the person in charge of researching Luke. "Go back to his place. Find out if he had an alibi for the night Lisa was attacked, and check it out. Don't just take his word for it."

The chief's phone rang from his belt, and he glanced at the caller. Answering the phone with his seemingly-favorite phrase, he said, "What've you got."

The room remained silent aside from the occasional "uh-huh" and "interesting" coming from the chief. After he hung up, he squeezed both hands into fists and placed them on the table, leaning forward. "That was Atkins. He's been looking into Lisa's whereabouts and the contacts she'd had with people over the past few weeks. Phone records indicate she'd been in contact with a male student from one of her classes." His eyes circulated the room. "A student by the name of Scott Sweigert, who happened to work at Jensen's drug store with Sonya Lee. Folks, we may have found ourselves a connection."

Zack and Jenny pulled into the parking lot of Jensen's Drug Store. "So, let me get this straight," Zack said. "Lisa was a pharmacology major, and she was in class with another pharmacology major who was interning at this drug store."

"Yes."

"And Sonya worked here as well."

"Yes, as a cahier in the pharmacy."

"Huh," was all Zack said. They got out of the car and headed toward the sliding double doors. "What are you hoping to find during this trip?"

"I'll know it when I see it," Jenny replied. "If I see it."

"Do you even know what this guy, Scott Sweigert, looks like?"

"Nope," Jenny confessed as they walked inside, "but maybe one of the girls will let me know."

Jenny wandered aimlessly through the store, but the only sensations she felt were familiarity and fondness. She believed those to be Sonya's emotions; she must have had fun working there. As Jenny worked her way around to the pharmacy counter in the back of the store, she saw photographs of the employees hanging on the wall. She scanned the pictures, noticing an empty spot. That must have been where Sonya's picture used to be. She looked around, finding the picture resting on the counter with a small shrine of flowers, cards and stuffed animals around it. She stared at the image for a moment, looking at the beautiful woman who smiled in her white lab coat. The picture was labeled with her given name, Song Yi, which Jenny found to be as lovely as the woman who owned it.

Jenny sighed and looked back at the collage of photos, searching for Scott Sweigert's picture, finding him a few spots down from the empty space. He was blond with glasses, looking rather average and nondescript. A ripple of both excitement and fear worked its way down Jenny's body as she remembered the detective who insisted the killer was someone ordinary. Scott Sweigert, it seemed, fit that description perfectly.

Jenny focused on the picture, trying to get some sort of reading from it. An image popped into her mind, leading her to close her eyes and allow the vision to run its course.

"You just don't try," she heard herself say in a friendly tone. "I refuse to feel sorry for you if you don't try."

She glanced to her left, seeing the profile of a smirking Scott Sweigert, who counted out pills on a tray. After accounting for them all, he poured them back into a container and replied, "You don't know what it's like. You're a girl. You don't have to do the asking. You're the one who gets asked."

"Well, that would never happen if every guy had your mindset, now, would it?"

"It's hard," he argued playfully.

"What's the worst that can happen? She says no. That's it."

"Okay, then," Scott said as he walked over toward Jenny at her register. He placed one hand on his hip and asked, "Will you go out with me?"

"Nope. I sure won't," Jenny replied in a chipper tone. "See, now that wasn't so bad, was it?"

He paused for a moment, smiled at her and replied, "No, it wasn't...but that's only because I didn't mean it. If I had been serious, that would have hurt."

Jenny glanced down and picked at her brightly painted fingernails. "It's all how you look at it. You can decide that your life sucks because *one girl* turned you down, or you can shrug it off knowing that she just wasn't the one."

"That's easy for you to say. You must have men asking you out all the time."

"Yeah, they're beating down my door."

"Didn't you just get asked out last week?"

"Yeah, by Jason. That hardly counts."

"It might to him."

"Can I help you?" The female voice was out of place. For a moment, Jenny was confused, but then she figured out the question had come from the present-day woman who stood behind the counter.

She had been frozen during the entire length of the vision; Jenny realized she must have looked like a crazy woman. "No, I'm just browsing, thank you." She smiled pleasantly, although she laughed at herself internally. What type of person browses by standing in one spot with her eyes closed?

Turning around, Jenny walked along the back of the store, glancing down each aisle in an attempt to find Zack. She discovered him in the magazine section and approached him with a giggle. "We need to get out of here before the pharmacist calls some guys with straitjackets to come get me."

"Made a good impression back there, huh?" Zack put the magazine back on the rack as they headed toward the exit.

"I got some information at least, even if it did cost me a little bit of pride."

"What did you find out?"

Jenny thought about the vision before flatly stating, "I don't know."

Zack let out a laugh. "That's not helpful."

"Well, I saw a conversation between Sonya and Scott, where Scott asked her out and she said no...although, it seemed to be a joke. Maybe. But then he mentioned that Sonya had been asked out by a guy named Jason, and she turned him down...adding that his invitation *hardly counted.*"

"Who is Jason? And why would his invitation not count?"

Jenny pulled her keys out of her purse as they reached the car. "I don't know...but I think we need to find out."

Chapter 5

Sitting in the driver's seat, Jenny noticed the rearview mirror reflected the roof of the car, not the back window. As she maneuvered it into place, she asked Zack, "Did you hit this thing on the way out?"

"I don't think so," he replied. "I'm pretty sure I didn't even come close to it."

With a shrug, she put the key in the ignition and started the car. With it still in park, Jenny dialed her phone, and soon the tiny detective's booming voice blared through the car speakers. "Brennan."

"Hi, Detective Brennan, it's Jenny Larrabee. I have a question for you. Has anyone by the name of Jason ever come up as a suspect?"

"Jason," she repeated as if she were thinking. "It doesn't sound familiar. Why? Did something happen involving a Jason?"

Jenny described the vision, concluding, "I'm not sure whether Sonya was trying to implicate Scott or Jason—or both. Considering she doesn't even know who did it, she may be grasping at straws herself."

"Well, Scott Sweigert is in the interrogation room as we speak. I'll make sure they get the message to ask who Jason is...that is, if they don't get a confession out of him first. I'm hoping they do, honestly—get a confession, that is. Then this whole thing will be over and the young women of this town can stop being afraid to go to sleep. This entire case has been a nightmare."

"I agree," Jenny replied. "Well, my plan for the day is to go to Buford Park and walk the trails...I want to see if any insight comes to me that way or if I can get an idea about what the deal is with that homeless man. Then I will go to the bars in the evening."

Zack chimed in, "I think we should go to the diner where Lisa Penne worked first. Maybe one of her coworkers or customers is the key to this whole thing. That, and I'm hungry."

Jenny rolled her eyes and shook her head. "I married a bottomless pit. Although, he may be on to something; going the diner is not a bad idea."

"Let me know if you're able to come up with anything," Detective Brennan said. "I'm going to get off the phone and call the guys doing the interrogation—let them know to ask about Jason."

"Sounds good," Jenny replied. They hung up, and she turned to her husband. "Do you know where the diner is?"

Pulling out his phone, he answered, "No, but I can find out."

Jenny stretched and thought about her baby as Zack looked up the information. She felt an ache in her stomach when she envisioned her mother holding her son, giving him the love that Jenny felt like she should have been giving. She had to admit she did enjoy the freedom that went along with not having the baby with her, a notion that made her feel even worse. What did that say about her as a mother?

She had no idea that motherhood would make her feel so conflicted.

Mercifully, Zack interrupted her thoughts. "It looks like the diner isn't that far from here. It's just a few blocks away."

"Cool," Jenny said as she put the car in reverse. "Which way should I go?"

"Well, considering it's a one-way street, you should head that way." He pointed in the only direction she could turn. "Then, once you hit Maple Street, you should take a left."

She followed Zack's instructions to the diner, which seemed to be a simple place that catered to college students. The square building was situated in the front portion of a plaza, leaving Jenny unsure which side was the front. "Where's the door? I have no idea where to park," she announced.

"It doesn't matter," Zack said. "Just pick a spot and we can walk."

Jenny pulled into one of the many available spaces, and the couple got out of the car. Soon, she realized why the lot had been so empty; she had parked in the back. "Sorry," she said with defeat. "Somehow I knew I'd get that wrong."

Zack only shrugged. After rounding the corner, a sign indicated they had reached the front of the diner, advertising that the restaurant was open twenty-four hours. As they walked up the three stone steps to the front door, Zack asked, "Can you imagine this place at three in the morning on a Saturday night? I bet it's crawling with drunks."

"Great," Jenny said sarcastically, pulling the door handle and walking in. "That'll help us narrow down the suspect pool. Holy mother of pearl, would you look at that?" She pointed to the dessert case at the front counter, which displayed an array of cakes and pies of every imaginable flavor. "I think I'll skip lunch and just climb right on into that thing. If you need me, I'll be behind the glass."

A waitress in all black approached them, grabbing a couple of menus and silverware rolls from behind a podium. "Two?" Her face seemed sullen, an appropriate look considering one of her coworkers had just been found murdered.

"Yes, please," Jenny replied politely. The couple was led to a booth along a window, where they got situated and the waitress walked away without a word.

"Are you getting anything?" Zack asked. "Readings, I mean, not lunch."

Jenny squinted as she focused on the feeling inside. "A little bit. There's a stir, but nothing definite." She looked around the diner, seeing a few men sitting alone at the counter. A wave washed over her, and the images of several faces flashed in her head in rapid succession. Each of them had been sitting at that very counter, but the view was from the other side—the employees' side, where Lisa had spent a good deal of time. "I take that back," Jenny added. "I've just gotten a glimpse at a handful of men."

Zack remained quiet for a moment before posing, "Any of them look promising?"

"No." Jenny shook her head. "She's guessing." More flashbacks ran through her mind—images of men sitting in booths, guys looking at her as she walked by. The visions came and went quickly, as if inspired by panic. Making a sound to voice her displeasure, Jenny admitted, "I don't like this very much."

"What's the matter? Do you need to leave?"

Once again, she shook her head. Releasing a controlled breath, she held up her hand and said, "No, I'm good." She took a stand inside her own mind, regaining some order, and the images came to an end. Still uneasy, she felt her hands tremble a bit as she began, "Do you know what this feels like to me?"

Zack shrugged and waited for her to continue.

"I imagine this is what it feels like to survive an attack."

At that moment, the waitress came by. After a quick glance at the menu, Zack and Jenny placed their orders and handed the menus back to the server. Once she left, Zack leaned forward onto his elbows. "What were you saying?"

"I was saying," Jenny continued, "that this is what it must feel like to be a survivor." Her eyes worked their way around the room, landing on each man that sat in the dining area. They all looked like murderers to her. She brought her attention back to her husband—the only male in the room she trusted. "I can imagine that the panic I'm feeling is what every survivor must experience. I mean, if a woman got attacked by a man in a mask and she has no idea who it was, she must look at every man differently after that. I see all these faces in here, and in my head, and I keep asking myself, *Is it him? Is it him? Is it him?*" She could no longer contain the shudder that sat just beneath the surface. "It's horrible."

"Yeah, that's got to be tough."

"It would be life-changing." She rested her chin in her hands. "I have to confess, I've had these crazy thoughts before. I've been alone in elevators with a male stranger, and it has occurred to me that the only reason he doesn't kill me is because he was raised right. I'm essentially trapped in there with him, and he's bigger than me, so I'm totally at his mercy if he's inclined to do anything violent. Now, for me, these thoughts are just random, unwarranted things that pop into my head. But for someone who has actually been attacked—and the person who did it is still out there—it would be entirely different. Maybe that stranger in the elevator is the attacker. Maybe he recognizes her as his victim and he wants to finish off what he started. Can you imagine how paralyzing that would be?"

"I think I would take the stairs," Zack replied.

"But being alone in a stairwell would be no different. The killer could just as easily get you in there." She leaned back in the booth, crossing her arms over her chest. "I've heard victims say they have to make an effort to reclaim their lives after they get assaulted, and I guess that's what they mean. They have to work at not being scared to take the elevator. Or the stairs. Or go anywhere alone, for that matter."

Drinks appeared before the couple. Zack took a sip of his coffee and remarked, "I'd probably get a gun and a permit to carry."

"My mom tried to encourage me to get a gun," Jenny announced as she shook a sugar packet, ripping it open and pouring it in.

"She did?"

After nodding and taking a drink, Jenny grunted her approval at the taste of the coffee. "Yeah. She wanted me to pick one up after she found out we brought Mick home with us to use the shower."

"Mick wasn't dangerous," Zack remarked.

"I told her that, but she didn't believe me. She just figured in our line of work we would run into some shady characters."

"We do run into some shady characters."

"I know," Jenny confessed, "but I still don't want a gun. I could never shoot anybody. I'd probably end up shooting myself as clumsy as I am sometimes. Besides, I'd want to keep it locked up with a child in the house, and I don't think an attacker would stand around and wait patiently while I got the key and opened the gun closet."

"Her point is valid, though. We get mixed up with murderers more often than your average couple."

"Well, this time we're dealing with a guy who likes co-eds who sleep alone, so I think I'm pretty safe." She reached down and fumbled around in her purse. "Speaking of my mother and Mick...I want to give each of them a call. I'd like to know how everybody's doing back home." She pulled her phone out and dialed her mother's number first.

Isabelle picked up after two rings. "Hello?"

"Hi, Ma. How's everything going?"

"Fabulous. Little man is sleeping right now."

Jenny's heart soared at the thought of her little baby snoozing away in his crib, making her wish she was there to see it. "Has he been doing okay?"

"He's doing fine. We've had fun; we went on a walk earlier today, and he made a little friend."

"He did?" Jenny could hardly contain herself. "Who?"

"A little sheltie who lives down the street."

She knew that dog; she had met the owners a few weeks before while on a walk. The sheltie had been quite curious about baby Steve, who didn't share the same enthusiasm about getting to know the dog. Still, Jenny beamed when she pictured the meeting.

"The dog kept sniffing his feet; it was very cute," Isabelle continued. "I imagine, in another couple of months, the baby will be enthralled with that little dog."

"He already is curious about Baxter," Jenny said, referring to her black lab mix at home. "He always looks at Bax when he walks by."

"Well, Baxter has a lot less fur to pull than this sheltie does."

Jenny bombarded her mother with questions about how much—and how well—Steve had been eating, sleeping, pooping and peeing. Zack winced when she engaged in the diaper talk with her mother, clearly less concerned than Jenny about the frequency of the baby's messy bottom. Once Jenny's fears had been eased and her curiosities satisfied, she got off the phone with her mom and looked over at Zack with a blank expression.

"What's that look about?" he asked.

"What look?"

"Exactly."

Jenny lowered her shoulders and explained, "I don't know what to feel. I'm both happy and sad at the same time."

"It sounds like the baby's doing well," Zack noted.

"He is...and that's what's making me sad. And happy."

Zack shook his head. "Women are complicated."

"We *are* complicated," Jenny agreed.

After blinking a few times, he asked, "Why would the fact that the baby is doing well make you sad?"

"Because he's doing well without me."

Zack remained both silent and motionless.

"Don't try to figure women out; you'll never get it. Just give me one more second...I have one other call to make, and then I'll stop being rude and I'll start paying attention to you."

She scrolled through her contacts until she found Mick's name, pressing the button to give him a call. He answered with a quiet, "Hey, Jenny."

"Hey." She lowered her eyebrows. "Is everything okay? You don't sound too happy about talking to me."

"It's that obvious, huh?"

Nearly overcome with a sense of fear, Jenny asked, "What's the matter?"

Mick released a long breath on the other end of the phone. "I'll feel like an asshole if I tell you," he said shamefully, "but I'll feel like an asshole if I don't."

"What happened?"

After an extended period of silence, he confessed, "I'm pretty sure John smoked crack the other night."

Jenny closed her eyes, feeling so disheartened by those words she could cry. "You're kidding me."

"I wish I was," he said with remorse, "but I would never joke about something like that."

"What happened?" Jenny looked across the table to see the concern on Zack's face. She held up a finger, instructing him to hang on while she waited for an explanation from Mick.

"I don't even know. I came home...two nights ago, I guess it was...and the house smelled funny. Like burnt plastic."

Jenny wiped her eyes; that's how John's house had smelled when she met him during the throes of his addiction.

Mick continued, "He was clearly acting strangely, and I figured he'd smoked something based on the smell of the house. I knew crack was his drug of choice, so I looked up what crack smells like, and the site said it does smell like burnt plastic."

"It does," Jenny replied with defeat.

Mick made a sound, expressing his unhappiness. "I didn't actually see him do anything, so I was reluctant to call you. I hoped that it was just some kind of misunderstanding. John and I have become pretty good friends over the past few months. He's a solid guy. I'd hate to see him fall back into his old ways."

"You and me both."

He let out a sigh. "I'm sorry I didn't call you as soon as it happened. I just didn't know what to do. It was one slip-up, and I wasn't sure if that meant he was on a bad path again or if it was an isolated incident. I'd hate to see him lose everything over one moment of weakness."

"He won't lose everything," Jenny assured him. "I won't give up on him that easily. But I also won't allow slip-ups. I'll make a phone call and let the testers know that he should be given a quote-unquote *random drug test* today." She sucked in a breath. "If he fails it, then he'll just need to go back to rehab for a while. That was part of our deal. He gets the house and the job and the insurance, but if any drug tests come back positive, he's got to get some help. In fact, he signed a document saying just that, and it's been notarized."

"So, he's not getting kicked out of the house?" Mick sounded guardedly optimistic.

"No, he's not getting kicked out. My goal is to help him; putting him out on the street won't accomplish that."

"Good," he replied with relief. "That makes me feel better."

"I'm glad," Jenny said. Putting some positivity in her tone, she asked, "And how are *you* doing?"

"I'm doing well. One day at a time, you know?"

"You're adjusting okay to living indoors?"

"Yeah. It does have its challenges, but the benefits are totally worth it. It's nice to be able to sleep at night with a locked door, knowing I'm safe. Sometimes, in the middle of the night, I wake up and I don't know where I am—I think I'm still on the street, or back in Iraq. It takes a minute for the reality to sink in, but it's nice when it does."

"Does Lucy sleep in bed with you?" Jenny asked, referring to the overly-timid pit bull she saved from euthanasia to give to Mick as a pet. "She was supposed to help with the nightmares."

"Lucy takes up more than half the bed," he said with a laugh, "and she snores. But, yes, she does help. When I start to freak out, it's nice just to have her with me. It calms me down."

"Excellent. I assume she's doing better, too?"

"She's comfortable here, in the house," Mick explained. "She is still painfully shy when we take her outside around strangers and other dogs, but she's getting better. Slowly."

"Good," Jenny said. "Is work going well?"

"Work is great," he replied. "It's nice to have a reason to get out of bed in the morning, and it's even better to have a *good* reason. I like being able to help people. *And,*" he added playfully, "it's led to something nice in my life. I have a girlfriend now."

Jenny felt her posture stiffen slightly. She had found herself attracted to Mick when she'd first met him; his sad, heroic story tugged at her heartstrings, especially since she and Zack were in a bad spot in their marriage at the time. Mick's bright blue eyes only added to the attraction. Now, here she was—four months later—feeling better in her marriage, but still a bit jealous at the prospect of Mick having a girlfriend. She liked it better when he was single, even if they couldn't be together.

Realizing how childish and selfish she was being, she plastered on a smile and said, "Really? Do tell."

"Her name is Samantha. She's Eddie Vincent's sister. Do you remember him?"

"Refresh my memory."

"He was the man who lost his vision in Afghanistan. You brought him to the intervention."

"Oh, yes, now I remember," Jenny said.

"Our first job was to make his house a talking house so he could function better. I met his sister when we were doing the renovation, and after a couple of months of friendship, we began dating."

With her petty jealousy fully in check, Jenny spoke sincerely. "That's great news. I'm happy for you. She's treating you well, I hope."

"Very," he said. "I have to admit, it's strange to be back in the dating scene. I don't really know what I'm doing, but she's very patient with me. I think watching her brother's struggle has helped her understand how difficult it is to resume a normal life after seeing combat."

This woman, whoever she was, was probably better for Mick than Jenny would ever be. "I'm glad to hear that. Truly. I wish you the best."

"Thanks. I really appreciate it."

Jenny let out a sigh. "Well, I guess I should get off the phone so I can call the drug testing folks and let them know they need to get out there. Don't worry...I won't tell anybody that you were the one who tipped me off. As far as John is concerned, he'll always just regard this drug test as a case of unfortunate timing."

"I appreciate that. I'd hate for him to feel like I betrayed him."

"Well, hopefully, after all of this is said and done, he will look back at this trip to rehab as a good thing and not see it as a *betrayal* at all. He probably won't be happy about it in the short term, but things that suck at the time often turn out to be the best things that ever happen to people."

"I hope that's true in this case."

"I'm hoping it will be." Jenny got off the phone with Mick and gave a quick call to the drug testing company. Their food arrived while she was talking to them, so she picked up her fork as soon as she put down her phone.

Zack spoke for the first time since the conversation with Mick. "I take it John's fallen off the wagon."

"It looks that way." Jenny's appetite had gone down after hearing the news, but she didn't want to waste the food. She took a half-hearted bite of her salad.

"That's a shame," Zack declared, eagerly placing a french fry in his mouth. "Although, I'm surprised it's taken this long."

"What are you talking about?"

He raised his eyes to look at her. "You didn't honestly think that he'd just be able to overcome a crack addiction without hitting any bumps in the road, did you?"

54

That was precisely what she had thought.

"He's going to battle these demons his whole life," Zack continued. "He'll never really be out of the woods."

But she'd helped him. She'd sent him to rehab, and fixed up his house, and sold it, and provided him with a new home with a friend to look out for him. He wasn't supposed to relapse.

"You're quiet," Zack said. "You're finding some way to blame yourself for this, aren't you?"

She stirred her salad around with her fork. "Maybe." After thinking about it some more, she added, "I guess I'm not really *blaming* myself. I'm just disappointed, that's all."

"Well, you should probably count on the fact that he's going to screw up from time to time—then it will be less upsetting when it happens." He took a big bite of his sandwich and tucked it into his cheek. "What was it your shrink said a few months ago? It's all about expectations?"

"You're right," she said. "Aim low, and I'm less likely to be let down."

"Atta girl," he replied. "Aim low…just like you did in your marriage." He flashed a playful grin.

She, too, managed a smile.

Once lunch was over, Zack and Jenny headed to the cash register to pay. Waiting in line for one other customer to finish settling her bill, Zack posed, "Where to now, chief? Buford Park?"

"I guess so," she replied. "I was hoping to hear back from Detective Brennan by now. It would have been nice if Scott Sweigert confessed; then we could just go home."

"I imagine she'd have called you by now if he confessed."

"I may not be at the top of her list of people to call," Jenny concluded. "I may not even be *near* the top."

"Well, assuming he didn't confess, shall we head to the park?" The people in line before them left, and Zack handed over the check and his credit card to the cashier. "If he didn't admit to anything, it would be a good place to look...and if he did turn himself in, then we can have a nice afternoon at the park." He looked at her and smiled.

"That's one way to look at it, I guess," Jenny said as she shrugged.

Once Zack signed the receipt, they headed out the door and down the steps. "Oh, that's right," Jenny began, "we parked out in no-man's-land."

"It's probably faster if we go the opposite way of how we came in."

"I think you're right."

The couple walked around the building as Jenny fished around her purse for a breath mint, mumbling to herself about being positive that she had some in there somewhere. Eventually, she heard Zack say, "Oh, shit."

She looked up. "What's the matter?"

Zack pointed to the car. "We have a flat tire. In fact," he added as he walked closer, "we have four." He circled the car, glancing up at Jenny with wide eyes. "Somebody slashed our tires."

Chapter 6

"What?" Jenny asked. "The tires have been *slashed*?"

"It looks that way. All of the tires have slices in them."

She immediately thought back to just a few hours before in the drug store parking lot, when the rearview mirror was pointed toward the roof of the car despite Zack saying he hadn't touched it. Fear engulfed her body in a giant wave. "I think someone is trying to send us a message."

"You think this was directed at us? You don't think this was random, shitty luck?"

Jenny shook her head, the rest of her body nearly paralyzed with fright. She reiterated the story about the rearview mirror. "The car wasn't locked then. I bet somebody went in there and messed with it, knowing we'd notice. And we'd certainly notice *this*." She shook her head more rapidly. "No, I think somebody's trying to tell us to back off this investigation."

"But how would they know ...oh, the Internet," Zack interrupted himself. "Your picture with the big headline."

"Exactly," Jenny replied, "and the car wouldn't be too hard to spot with Tennessee plates."

"That's scary," he said. "That would mean the person followed us from the pharmacy."

Jenny looked around the parking lot, unable to find anything or anyone who stood out. "Do you think he's still watching us?"

"I don't know," Zack admitted. "One thing I do know is that I'm not letting you go anywhere alone."

As the initial fear started to wear off, Jenny thought rationally for a moment. "This guy likes to attack women who are alone and asleep. Do you really think we're in danger? Or do you think this guy just wants us to go home so we don't figure out who he is?"

"I can't say…but either way, we can't be careless. There's too much at stake."

Jenny nodded as she leaned against the hood of the car, the helplessness of the moment sinking in. "Okay, so, now what?"

"Now," Zack began as he pulled out his phone, "we call a tow truck."

"How long will that take?"

"No idea. We'll need a flat-bed; that might make things a little trickier." He tapped and swiped his phone as Jenny realized this was shaping up to be a long and boring afternoon.

She scooted up onto the hood, placing her feet on the front fender. Sinking her chin into her hands, she felt a slight tingle in her chest, giving her an unfortunate reminder. "Uh oh," she said. "I'm going to need to use my pump at some point, and it's back at the hotel."

Zack raised his eyes to look at her and then went back to his phone. "We'll figure something out," he replied. "How soon do you need it?"

"Within an hour or so."

"I'll make sure you have it by then." After a few phone calls, he eventually announced, "They said they can have someone out here in forty-five minutes to an hour. I'll call a cab to take me back to the hotel so I can get the pump."

"Wouldn't it make more sense for me to go back to the hotel and just pump while I'm there?"

"By yourself? No. You can stay here, where you'll be surrounded by people. I'll just bring it to you. Is everything you need in the case?"

"Yeah, it's all there." Jenny smiled at him. "Thank you."

"No problem. I may have to turn in my man card for this one, though."

"No," she protested, "a real man protects his wife, even if it means carrying a breast pump."

Zack grumbled something inaudible, then said, "I'm just glad we're in a different state and I won't run into anybody I know." He called a cab company, stating his location, and turned to Jenny once he hung up. "Why don't we go back inside? The driver will probably pull up to the front of the diner anyway, and it'll be safer in there with all those people around."

She hated the idea of having to strategize in order to be safe, but she agreed to wait for the cab inside. They wordlessly walked back into the diner, where their waitress looked at them funny. "Car trouble," Zack explained. She lost interest and went about her business.

"Something's weird," Jenny announced, inspired by a buzzing inside her stomach.

"What?" Zack asked.

"I don't know. Something."

Jenny found herself drawn into the dining section of the restaurant, her eyes landing on a middle-aged man sitting by himself in a booth. He looked harmless enough—slightly overweight with glasses and graying hair—but Jenny's attention was definitely being brought to him.

"What is it?" Zack said quietly from behind her.

A whisper of a name echoed through Jenny's head. "I can't say for sure," she began, "but I'm pretty sure we just found our mystery guy, Jason."

"Jason..." Zack reiterated, "you mean the guy who had asked out Sonya Lee? The one she was talking to Scott Sweigert about?"

"I believe so," Jenny remarked with a distant nod. She inconspicuously raised her finger in the middle-aged man's direction.

Zack looked in his direction. "He's, like...old." There was disgust in his voice.

"Maybe that's why Sonya said his invitation didn't count."

"He's wearing a wedding ring."

"Reason number two." Jenny turned around and announced, "I don't want to stare at the guy, especially if he's the one who just slashed our tires."

"Okay, now I don't feel so good about leaving you here while I go back to the hotel."

"It's a public place," she replied with a shake of her head. "I'll be fine." She looked at a table of what appeared to be construction workers eating lunch, feeling validated. "He can't do anything to me here."

Zack's eyes focused over her shoulder, fixated on Jason. "He seems pretty nonchalant," he remarked. "He either doesn't know we're here, he's not our guy, or he's a pretty good actor."

Jenny turned back around slowly, looking at the man with just her eyes. He appeared to be flirting with the waitress who had just arrived at his table, exuding a big smile and demonstrating playfulness in his eyes. The waitress was half his age.

"Check out Casanova," Zack remarked. "Look, she doesn't even seem to be repulsed by him."

"She works for tips," Jenny noted.

"True."

The couple watched him in action as the waitress walked away and he began to read a book. "I'll get a table while you're gone," Jenny began. "You said we had, what, forty-five minutes before the tow truck would come?"

"Thereabouts."

"I have time to grab dessert, then. I'll stay in the dining area and see if anything comes to me."

"A waitress should come to you," Zack replied. "You can ask her about this guy and see if she thinks he'd make a good suspect."

Jenny nodded. "I'll do that."

"Are you sure you're okay in here by yourself?"

"I'm not by myself. I'll be fine."

"Okay, then, I guess I'll wait out front for the cab. In my experience, if they pull up and you're not there, they leave." The couple said their goodbyes; he kissed her on the cheek and headed out the door.

Jenny flagged down one of the waitresses as she walked by. "Excuse me," Jenny began, "is it okay if I take a seat again? We're having car trouble, and the tow truck won't be here for a while."

"Sure thing, sweetie. Just give me a second, and I'll seat you." The woman disappeared for a moment, returning to lead Jenny to a booth.

"I think *the powers that be* are telling me I should get dessert," Jenny told the woman as they weaved through the tables.

"That's how I'd interpret it," the waitress replied with an artificial smile, leaving a menu and a roll of silverware at Jenny's table. "Julie will be right with you," she announced monotonously before walking away.

The mood at the diner definitely reflected the previous day's events; Lisa was evidently going to be missed at the diner.

Jenny looked at the back page of the giant menu, trying to decide on just one dessert when they all looked so good. She periodically glanced up at Jason, who sat motionlessly reading his book. He didn't seem to be the least bit agitated, which Jenny would have expected if he'd just slit her tires. Although, if he had been capable of killing two women, he probably wouldn't have thought twice about poking a few holes in some rubber.

Julie arrived at the table, introducing herself and asking Jenny if she was ready to order. "I'm not yet," Jenny confessed, "I can't figure out which dessert I want…but I'd like to ask you a few questions, if you don't mind."

"Sure," Julie replied. "What would you like to know?"

"That guy over there." Jenny nudged her head in Jason's direction. "The one reading the book."

The waitress looked behind her, turning back and saying, "Yeah?"

"What's his story?"

"Jason?" she asked. "He's a regular here."

"Anything remarkable about him?"

"Other than the fact that he flirts relentlessly with every one of the waitresses?"

"Does he ever ask the waitresses out?"

"Often," she replied with a playful snort.

"Do you think he's serious when he asks?"

"Nah, he's just joking around."

"Is he married? I see he has a ring on."

"I think so," she replied, "but we've never seen his wife in here." She looked intently at Jenny for a moment before asking, "What is this about? Are you interested in him or something?"

That question was the last thing Jenny had expected to hear. "What? Interested? No." She shook her head. Softening her tone to reflect sympathy, she added, "I am just trying to see if he might have had anything to do with what happened to Lisa."

The mention of Lisa's name caused the waitress put her hand to her mouth and close her eyes for a long moment, looking as if she was battling tears.

"I'm sorry," Jenny said. "I don't mean to upset you. I just want this solved, and I have reason to believe he also asked out the other victim, Sonya Lee, while she was at work at Jensen's drug store." Julie didn't respond, so Jenny continued, "Do you think he'd be capable of such a thing?"

"I don't know," Julie replied with a shaky voice. "I don't know anything anymore."

"I'm sure the police have already interviewed you," Jenny deduced.

"At length."

"Did you have any suspects in mind?"

She shook her head solemnly. "I was under the impression it was random. I even told the police that. Lisa couldn't possibly have had any enemies. She was so sweet and fun-loving." A tear worked its way down Julie's cheek; she wiped it away with the back of her hand.

"Again, I'm really sorry," Jenny said sincerely. "I don't mean to bring up something so horrible; I just want to make sure it doesn't happen again."

With closed eyes, Julie simply nodded.

"So, you don't think it could have been Jason?"

"I doubt it. He's been coming in here and flirting with the waitresses for over a year. Why would he all of a sudden kill one of us? I mean, why now?"

Why now? Jenny thought. A valid question indeed. "Just one more thing, and then I'll leave you alone." she said. "Do you know his last name?"

"It's Lewis," the waitress said. "Jason Lewis."

"Great." Jenny held the menu up in Julie's direction. With positivity in her voice, she added, "I'll tell you what. Why don't you just surprise me with a dessert? Bring me your favorite...I'm sure I'll love it."

Julie nodded, returning to her professionalism. "Got it. One mystery dessert, coming right up." She took the menu and walked away.

Jenny rested her head in her hands, thinking about the timing, the question, 'why now?' burning in her brain. What had happened to trigger this violence? With two murders so sudden and close together, something must have recently set the killer off. Either that, or he was new to the area and the killings were just the two latest in a series of unsolved murders that had begun somewhere else.

Armed with a last name and a curiosity that got the best of her, Jenny dialed the detective, hearing the distinctive, "Brennan," on the other end of the line.

"Hi, Detective Brennan, it's Jenny Larrabee." She lowered her voice to make sure nobody could hear her. "I think I have discovered the identity of the mysterious Jason."

"You mean Jason Lewis?" she asked.

"You already know?"

"Scott Sweigart told us his name, but little else," Detective Brennan explained. "Scott was willing to admit that Jason was a regular customer of the pharmacy and often flirted with Sonya, but he wouldn't explain why Jason came to the drug counter so often. He cited confidentiality and said he wouldn't disclose anything about Jason's reason for being there without a subpoena."

"I'm assuming Scott didn't confess, then?"

"Not even close. I think *vehement denial* is a better term. He insisted that it was just an unfortunate coincidence that his coworker and the girl he hoped to date were both selected as victims. I don't know, though. That's an awfully big coincidence in my book."

"Well, it sounds like Jason Lewis flirts with everybody he sees, so it may be a coincidence that he hit on both girls, too."

"Wait," Detective Brennan said, "Jason flirted with Lisa, too?"

"He's apparently a regular customer at Athens Diner, where Lisa worked. In fact, he's here right now."

"He's there now?"

"Sure is."

"Keep him there," Detective Brennan commanded. "I can be there in five minutes." She hung up without saying goodbye.

Jenny finished off the last bite of her Boston Crème pie, which tasted every bit as good as it looked, just as Detective Brennan came into the diner. The detective didn't explain herself as she walked past the hostess stand, taking a quick seat across from Jenny in the booth. "He still here?" she asked.

With a nod, Jenny sipped her water and made a sound of affirmation. After swallowing, she gestured in Jason's direction, saying, "Yup. Navy blue jacket."

Detective Brennan looked over her shoulder at the seemingly innocuous man, who sat alone eating a sandwich. "Excellent." She turned back to Jenny. "I think we should go over and have a little discussion with him, no?" She started to get up.

"Now?" Jenny asked with surprise. "You don't want to bring him into the station?"

"He's not a suspect...yet," the detective explained. "I just want to ask him some questions. Considering he was affiliated with both victims, he should find the request to be reasonable." She stood up, flashing Jenny a look. "You coming?"

"You want me over there?"

"Of course I do," she replied. "You have insight that no one else has. Besides," she added with a smirk, "that's how the chief wants it."

"But..." Jenny remained in her seat. She felt reluctant to disclose this information, but she felt like it needed to be said. "Somebody slashed my tires, and I am afraid it might be him."

The grin immediately left the detective's face. "Somebody slashed your tires? When?"

"Just now. My car is out in the parking lot with four flats. That's why I'm still here—I can't leave."

"Did you report this?"

"I guess I am now," Jenny said.

Looking back at the man who still had half of a sandwich left to eat, Detective Brennan sat back down, pulling out a notepad. "Can you give me a timeframe?"

"Well, Zack and I stopped briefly at Jensen's Drug Store after the meeting got out this morning, and then we came here. We went to leave about fifteen minutes ago, give or take. Somewhere in between, our tires got slashed."

She jotted down the information. "And when did Jason come in?"

Jenny sighed as she thought about the question. "I am thinking he came in while we were outside. I didn't see him before that, but I guess it's possible that I just overlooked him." After mulling the idea over some more, she added, "Do you think he'd come in here and eat lunch after slashing my tires? I would imagine he'd want to leave as quickly and discretely as he could if he was guilty."

The detective shook her head. "Not necessarily. Do you remember the DC snipers? I know of at least one instance where they shot their victim in a restaurant parking lot and then went in and had dinner. While the police were frantically searching every road that led away from the scene, the snipers were hanging out nonchalantly inside." She scoffed, adding, "It didn't help that the cops were looking for a lone Caucasian in a white van when the perps were two African Americans in a blue Chevy Caprice, but that's beside the point."

This story was not making Jenny feel any better. "Do you think it's safe for me to go over there?"

"It will be when I call for backup." Detective Brennan used her cell phone to request additional officers. Despite this, Jenny still felt nervous. "But if he slit my tires because he doesn't want me investigating anymore, wouldn't it be bad for me to confront him?"

"If he slit your tires because he doesn't want you investigating anymore, that means he already knows you're investigating to begin with, now, doesn't it?"

Jenny imagined this tiny woman didn't get to where she was on the force by being afraid. With an emphatic nod, Jenny said, "You're right. I guess I've got nothing to lose."

The two women approached the booth where the nondescript man sat. Detective Brennan took immediate charge of the situation. "Jason Lewis?"

He looked up with a mixture of curiosity and apprehension as he wiped his mouth with a napkin. "Yes?"

"Detective Brennan," she replied, pulling a badge out of her pocket and flashing it quickly, "and this, as you may or may not know, is Jenny. Can we have a seat, sir?"

He gestured to the other side of the booth with his hand. "Be my guest." As the women got situated with Jenny's heart beating a mile a minute, he added, "Is this, by any chance, about what happened to Sonya and Lisa?"

"In fact, it is," Detective Brennan said.

"Terrible, isn't it?" The sadness in Jason's eyes looked genuine. "They were both so young and so sweet." He shook his head.

"You were familiar with both of them, correct?"

"Yes, I was. I am a regular both here and at Jensen's."

"I can understand being a regular here," she replied, matter-of-factly, "but what would be your purpose for repeatedly visiting the pharmacy counter at Jensen's Drug Store?"

He looked slightly offended by the question. "I'm picking up medication."

"For a condition?" Detective Brennan asked.

Jason wore a serious expression as he replied, "For my wife." Jenny couldn't help but feel like he was being defensive.

"Yes, your wife. About that," Detective Brennan began. "I do see you are wearing a wedding ring, and you openly admit you are married, but I have reports that you repeatedly ask out all of the waitresses here…including Lisa Penne…who, as you know, was found murdered. I also have witnesses telling me you had been known to ask out Sonya Lee. Do you care to explain that?"

Sitting back in the booth, Jason replied, "Oh my God; you think I did this."

"I don't think anything," Detective Brennan replied. "I would just like to know why a married man asked out two women who both ended up dead."

"You think I was serious when I asked them out? I flirt with all the young women. It's harmless...all in good fun."

"Would your wife agree to that statement?"

"My *wife* can't agree to anything. She can't even speak." Anger and irritation turned to sadness before Jenny's eyes. Jason sighed with defeat, lowering his shoulders, softly admitting, "She has advanced stage Huntington's Disease."

The edge left Detective Brennan's voice as she said, "I'm sorry...I'm not familiar with Huntington's Disease."

"It's in the same family as Parkinson's and ALS. It's degenerative and adult-onset." His eyes rose to meet the detective's. "And horrible."

If the story had tugged at Detective Brennan's heartstrings, she didn't show it. "So, you go to the pharmacy frequently to pick up your wife's medication?"

He nodded slowly. "I still take care of her, but I don't know how much longer I'm going to be able to do that. She needs round-the-clock care as it is."

"But you're here..." Detective Brennan said.

"Yes, I'm here." Jason looked down at the table. "I have nurses come in so I can take a break from time to time. I know it sounds silly...I took leave from my job so I could care for my wife full time. I don't work...how is it that I should need a break?"

"It doesn't sound silly at all," Jenny said compassionately. "I have a baby, and as much as I love him, I still need time away from him once in a while...time where I can just be me and not have to worry about watching him."

Jason sighed and looked at Jenny, who admittedly felt no fear when they locked eyes. "Exactly," he agreed. "I love my wife, but it's so hard to hook up the feeding tube of a woman who once wowed me with her intelligence." His eyes grew distant. "She was brilliant, once upon a time."

"How is it you are able to get away with not working?" Detective Brennan asked. "I assume you've got some hefty medical bills."

Snapping back into the present, Jason said, "Huntington's disease isn't the only thing that runs in her family...that brilliance does, too. Her father was a highly successful biochemist who lost his wife to the disease. He wanted to make sure his daughter was well cared for at the end, so he gave me enough money to take an extended leave of absence from work once her symptoms got bad. I've been trying to live up to that expectation, but it's hard. It's like watching her live in purgatory." He cleared his throat. "I just need to get away sometimes."

Jason's attention was drawn toward the front door of the diner, causing Jenny to glance back over her shoulder. Three uniformed police officers had entered and were talking to the hostess. One of them pointed toward the booth where the trio sat. Jason's eyes quickly landed on Detective Brennan, looking as if he felt betrayed. "I thought you said you didn't suspect me."

"It's probably about me," Jenny said quickly. "My tires were slashed in the parking lot. They might be coming to investigate."

Bitterness remained on Jason's face. "They wouldn't send three cops to investigate vandalism...not when there are women being murdered. They wouldn't waste the resources." He sat back in the booth once again, folding his arms across his chest. "Tell me what this is really about. I'm a suspect, aren't I?"

Detective Brennan spoke deliberately. "You are not a suspect. We are just investigating every angle, and we know that you have flirted with..."

"For the love of God," he said through gritted teeth, "I am a man with a very sick wife. I have remained one-hundred percent faithful to her, even though she's been incapacitated for over a year now. Yes, I go out and flirt with other women. I'm still alive, after all. But that doesn't make me a murderer—it just makes me human."

Jenny couldn't help but feel that the only decent thing to do at that point would have been to walk away.

However, Detective Brennan continued, "Just one more question…what size shoe do you wear?"

"Nine and a half wide."

Glancing under the table, the detective nodded with verification.

"You want to take my shoes with you?" he asked bitterly. "You can. You can also polygraph me, take my blood, my fingerprints, my DNA…I've got nothing to hide. Maybe all that will show you I didn't do it."

"None of that will be necessary," Detective Brennan replied, "for now." She began to scoot out of the booth as she asked, "Do you have any scheduled trips out of town in the upcoming weeks?"

"My wife has Huntington's; I'm not going anywhere."

"Well, then, Mr. Lewis, I won't keep you any longer. Thank you for the information. We'll be in touch if it becomes necessary."

He responded only by following her movements with his eyes as she stood.

Jenny stayed behind as the detective headed toward the front door. Hoping she had successfully portrayed herself as the "good cop," she extended her hand to Jason and said, "I wish you the best. I have to say, I admire your dedication to your wife. I know a lot of people wouldn't be able to do what you are doing."

He looked at her for a moment before accepting her offer. Shaking her hand, he simply replied, "Thank you."

Her hand didn't burn from the contact.

Chapter 7

"I don't know how this works," Jenny confessed as she and Zack sat in the lobby of the tire store. "My hand didn't burn when I touched Jason, but I am not sure of why that happens in the first place. In the past, when I have made contact with a killer, I can feel it...but is that because the victim knows who their murderer is and they're letting me know? Or will I always feel that burning sensation if I come in contact with someone who has taken a life?"

"That would be cool if it were true," Zack observed. "You could just walk around touching everyone. You could have a cop with handcuffs with you, and if your hand burned, you could just tell the cop, 'Arrest this one.'"

"Um, this is America," Jenny replied. "I'm not sure things work that way here."

Zack shrugged a shoulder. "It would still be cool."

Jenny shook her head, freeing her mind of that thought. "It could be that Jason actually did do it, but if Lisa and Sonya don't know that, my hand wouldn't have burned when I touched him."

"So, in other words, this tells you very little."

"Well, if it turns out he did do it, then I know the burn thing only works when the victims are aware of their killer. Although," she added with a twisted face, "his shoes were the wrong size. By a lot. I mean, I can understand wearing a different sized shoe to commit a crime in order to throw the investigators off, but five sizes? That would be like wearing clown shoes. Besides, do you really think he could climb through a window? He wasn't exactly the picture of fitness."

"I'm assuming, then, that you don't think he did it."

Blowing out an exhale, she confessed, "No, I really don't."

"That makes two of the three," Zack said. "You don't believe it was Luke Thomas, either. Does that mean the number one suspect in your mind is Scott Swiegart?"

"I'd have to meet him first before I can decide on that."

"It is a bit strange that he works with Sonya and was apparently trying to date Lisa...don't you think?"

"He's either guilty or he's one of the unluckiest guys in the world."

The two sat in silence as they each toyed with their phones. Glancing at her husband, Jenny remarked, "Do you realize I pumped breast milk in the bathroom of a diner?"

"Classy," Zack replied.

"And then I rode in a tow truck with a breast pump on my lap," she added with a frown. "What on earth happened to my pride?"

"If it makes you feel any better, the driver probably didn't know it was a breast pump," Zack said. "It looks like an ordinary black case; they do a pretty good job of disguising it, actually. I bet the driver was more worried about it being a bomb."

"Why would I want to blow up a tow truck?"

"Why would some dude slit the throats of sleeping college students?"

"Touche." Jenny's mind switched from how little pride she had to the motivation behind the killer's actions. "The waitress at the diner said something that struck me...she said, *Why now?* Why all of the sudden would this person start killing college girls? Something must have happened to trigger him."

"Maybe his meds got changed."

Jenny let out a sigh. "We would never know that unless we caught him and asked him that."

"Exactly," Zack replied. "There very well may have been a trigger, but we may not know what it was until after we catch this guy."

Jenny's phone rang in her hand; she answered it with a quick, "Hello?"

"Jenny. Detective Brennan. You got a minute?"

"Unfortunately, I have lots of minutes. We're getting new tires put on. What's up?"

"We looked around the neighboring businesses, seeing if anyone had a security camera pointed in the direction of your car. I was hopeful that we could get a look at the perpetrator, and maybe that's the guy we're looking for in the Lee and Penne cases."

"Were you able to find one?" Jenny's heart began to beat a little faster.

"Afraid not," she replied. "The place that you parked—behind the diner but far away from the other stores—is one of the few places in the lot that isn't monitored."

"Great," Jenny muttered. "What about Jensen's Drug Store?"

"They have a camera, but—believe it or not—it isn't working."

Wiping her eyes with her free hand, Jenny replied with only a sigh.

"Yeah, I was disappointed, too," the detective announced. "Just do me a favor and be careful. If this is our guy, we know what he's capable of."

"All too well," she said. "Don't worry; I'll be safe. I won't go anywhere alone."

She hung up the phone, and after a few minutes she heard the man behind the counter announce, "Honda Civic?"

"I think that's our cue," Zack said to Jenny as they stood up and headed to the counter.

The mechanic told the couple about what he had done, summarizing the charges. "It's a shame," he added. "Those old tires still had a lot of life left in them."

"I know," Jenny replied. "I just got them not too long ago."

"So, what happened?" the man asked with a smirk as he swiped Zack's credit card. "Did you piss somebody off?"

"It's distinctly possible," Jenny said. If only the man knew.

"Are you a teacher or something? Is some kid angry about an F?"

"Somebody's definitely angry," she replied. "We just don't know about what."

"It's sad that whole ordeal took so long," Jenny noted as she and Zack looked for parking space on Center Street, where the three bars were housed. "We totally missed our opportunity to go to the park."

"Tomorrow," Zack replied. "We can go in the morning."

Jenny nodded as she found a vacant spot. "I know; it's just a complete waste of an afternoon dealing with flat tires. We could have been much more productive with our time."

"Well, somebody had other designs for our day...and they won."

The exited the car, looking at the nearly empty street in front of them. The three popular bars were all within sight, on the same side of the street with some small businesses in between. "Where do you want to start?" Zack asked.

"I seem to remember that Shenanigans was Lisa's favorite; maybe we should start there."

"That sounds good. The only problem is that it's only eight o'clock. That's like noon to these college kids. They probably won't even hit the bars until ten or so."

"Maybe that's not such a bad thing," Jenny replied. "If it's nearly empty, I may be able to get a better reading. If it's crawling with people, there may be too much going on for me to get the messages the girls are trying to send."

"Well, then, by all means." He gestured his arm in the direction of Shenanigans, inviting Jenny to lead the way.

As they approached the door, a large man dressed in a black t-shirt with a Shenanigans emblem held out his arm, blocking their path. "Hang on a minute," he said. "I need to see IDs."

"Really?" Jenny asked, feeling both flattered and surprised. "Don't I look old enough?"

"We card everyone, ma'am," the bouncer replied. "House rule."

"Dude," Zack began, "you were better off saying she looked young."

The bouncer laughed. "You're right. Duly noted." He held up Jenny's license to the light, saying, "Tennessee, huh? What brings you here to ole Bennett, Missouri?" He handed her card back to her.

"Investigation, actually," Jenny replied as he checked Zack's license as well. "We're looking into the murders that have happened here recently, and we're retracing the girls' steps."

"Yeah," he said with a shake of his head, "both girls used to come in here quite a bit. They were regulars."

"Do you know of anyone who might have had their eye on them? Anyone who appeared suspicious?"

He shook his head. "I usually only work the door. I see them come in; I see them go out. Whatever happens in between is on someone else's watch."

"Did they ever leave with the same guy?" Zack asked.

The bouncer shrugged. "So many people leave here in pairs, only to leave in different pairs the next week. It's too hard to keep track of."

Jenny smiled. "Well, thanks for your help."

"Good luck to you, ma'am," he replied.

After taking a few steps toward the doorway, Jenny turned to Zack and whispered, "When did I become a ma'am?"

"Probably around the time you gave birth."

They opened the door, revealing a long, skinny room that went back much deeper than Jenny had expected. The bar extended about halfway down the right wall, with very little room to stand to the left of it. Behind the bar, some booths and high-top tables were positioned in front of a small stage, which currently didn't feature a band. The unnecessarily loud music currently came through the speakers, and the room smelled of stale beer.

Leaning over so she could be near Zack's ear, she yelled, "People actually like this place?"

"College kids? Sure," he replied, equally as loudly. "They have different standards than you do, ma'am."

"I guess I *am* old," she admitted with a frown. "I can't see the attraction to this place."

"Alcohol, music and a room full of potential mates," Zack declared. "It's pretty much all they need at that age."

"I wasn't that way," Jenny said.

"You were the exception."

"My feet are sticking to the floor."

"Focus on the mission."

Zack was right; Jenny needed to remember her purpose for being there. Tucking her disgust away, she asked, "Shall we go have a seat?"

"After you."

She headed to the booth in the corner, where the music was quieter and she could actually hear herself think. "One of the guys at the meeting this morning said that Luke Thomas hangs out here quite a bit."

"He's that tall guy who lives upstairs from Sonya, right?"

Jenny nodded. "Although," she added, "I wouldn't think the star basketball player would drink that much. Wouldn't that be detrimental to his athletic career?"

"Maybe," Zack said with a shrug. "It's not like Perdion University is a huge contender for the final four or anything. He might still tie one on from time to time."

"Greg didn't drink that much because he was a running back," Jenny noted, referring to her first husband. "But he may have over-emphasized the importance of that role in his own head." Looking around, she added, "I don't know why anyone would want to hang out here if they're not drinking, though."

"Girls," Zack said flatly.

"Aren't there girls all over campus? Why would Luke need to come here for girls?"

"The girls here are drunk. That's a big help for a guy looking to hook up."

"Luke's a good-looking kid, and he's an athlete. I bet he has girls falling all over him."

Zack shrugged. "Alcohol still makes it easier."

A waitress approached them, asking if they wanted anything to eat or drink. "You have food here?" Zack asked.

"Yup," the waitress replied. "It's all listed on the card."

In the center of the table, a stand displayed a list of all of the available appetizers. After a quick look, Zack said, "I'll have an order of nachos and a Sam Adams."

"We just had dinner," Jenny said with a mixture of awe and disgust. "How can you possibly..." She held up her hand, stopping herself. This was Zack, after all. He could eat anything at any time. "I'll just have a water, please," she told the waitress, who then turned and walked away.

"So, are you getting any feelings or anything?"

"Not yet," Jenny said, "but I haven't tried that hard."

"Why don't you give it a whirl? I've got to hit the head anyway."

Jenny nodded as Zack got up and walked away. She closed her eyes, leaning back in her seat, allowing herself to fully relax. A funny feeling washed over her as three fashionable college girls appeared in the booth around her, each wearing a bright smile.

"How are you ladies doing tonight?" A dark-haired young man had approached the table, beer in hand. He looked as if he'd been drinking heavily.

One of the girls looked up at him, saying, "We're doing fine. How about yourself?"

"I'm doing great. You all look like you could use a refill."

Jenny glanced down at the nearly-empty cup in her hand, her bright nail polish showing despite the dim lighting. "We *are* running a little low," she announced.

"What are you drinking?" the man asked. "I'll fill your pitcher."

"Yuengling," a blond girl replied flirtatiously.

Reaching over and grabbing the empty pitcher from the table, the man said, "Yuengling it is. I'll be right back."

With half-closed eyes, one of the girls turned to the blond and said, "We're not drinking Yuengling."

"We are if we're not paying for it," the blond replied.

"You do realize he's going to expect somebody's phone number for this," Jenny heard herself say.

The blond shrugged. "That's his problem. Just because he buys us a pitcher, that doesn't mean we owe him a date. It's how the game goes."

"Well, then, here's to the game," one of the girls proposed.

The four young women raised their plastic cups to the center of the table. "To the game!" they all agreed, finishing their drinks in one giant gulp.

The girls disappeared, leaving Jenny by herself in the booth in the nearly-deserted bar. She wiped her hands down her face, realizing this was going to be a complicated case to solve. With alcohol thrown into the mix, the suspect pool just became immeasurably larger.

Zack returned, taking his seat across from her. "Any luck?" he asked.

"Of sorts," she replied, telling his about her latest vision. "It seems Sonya was a bit of a partier."

"How do you know it was Sonya?"

"The hands," she said. "Sonya always wore fluorescent nail polish, so it's easy for me to figure out who's who. But if Sonya and her friends were willing to accept the drinks men bought them and then reject the guys at the end of the night, that could have very easily made somebody angry."

"If I remember it right, Sonya was killed on a weeknight, after she had spent the night at home studying," Zack said. "If that was the trigger for this guy, it wasn't a knee-jerk reaction. He must have remembered her, figured out where she lived and planned it."

A thought occurred to Jenny, causing her to stand up and announce, "I'll be right back."

Trotting off toward the door, Jenny noticed the music got louder and louder, almost reaching the point of being painful. Once again, she struggled to see the draw of this place.

Mercifully, the sound disappeared once she got outside and the door closed behind her. She approached the bouncer who sat on a stool, looking bored. "Excuse me," she said, "I'm sorry to bother you."

He smiled at her. "You're not bothering anything. There's nothing to bother at this point."

"When does it normally get busy?"

"It becomes steady around ten-thirty."

"That's my bedtime," Jenny announced with a giggle. "No wonder you called me ma'am."

"Not a partier?" he asked.

"I wasn't even a partier back when I was supposed to be one. I do have a question for you, though, if you don't mind."

"Ask away."

"What's it like when people leave here? Like, do they often leave all at once, in a big herd or something?"

"Well, people stagger out of here throughout the night, but when closing time hits, which is two in the morning, there is mass exodus."

"And a lot of the people who leave here are drunk?"

"That's a bit of an understatement."

Jenny looked around at the street, noticing her car was one of the few parked there. "Do they drive home?"

"Generally not," the bouncer replied. "A lot of the campus housing is within walking distance."

"Doesn't it get cold here in the middle of the winter at two in the morning?"

"Yup, but they don't care," he replied. "Put enough alcohol in them, and they don't feel the cold."

"You probably do, sitting out here," she said with a smile.

"When it gets real bad, I stand inside the doorway."

"Okay, so, when the kids leave, is it peaceful? Rowdy? Loud?"

"It depends on the night. Sometimes it's uneventful, other nights I'm breaking up brawls."

"Do you think a group of girls could be followed home without noticing?"

"Easily."

Easily.

A trio of young men approached the door, so Jenny said, "I'll get out of your way. Thanks for your help."

"No problem," the guy replied before turning his attention to the customers.

Jenny walked back into the bar, through the blaring music and back to her husband, who was sipping on a beer while playing with his phone. He glanced up at her, asking, "Did you find out anything?"

"Only the stark realization that it could have been anybody." She plopped into the booth, adding, "This strip of bars is only a handful of blocks from both Sonya's and Lisa's places. It's within walking distance, if you wanted to avoid driving home. According to the bouncer, most people do walk after leaving here, and it would be very easy to follow a group of drunk girls out of here without them noticing." She wiped her eyes. "It may have been a quick, casual encounter that sealed these girls' fates. They may have simply rejected the wrong guy." Hanging her head, she muttered, "This is turning into a nightmare."

A plate of nachos appeared before Zack, who thanked the waitress and began digging in. Still full from dinner, Jenny almost felt sick watching him eat again.

"Well, there is that one piece of concrete evidence," Zack noted, "that size fourteen shoe print outside Lisa's window. You know who probably has feet that big? Luke Thomas."

"I know," Jenny replied with a sigh. "Jason Lewis—the guy with the sick wife—had much smaller feet than that. I don't know about Scott Sweigert."

"I think you'd have to be a pretty big guy to have feet that size."

"Either that, or you'd have to be freakishly disproportionate."

"Do you know how tall Scott is?"

"Based on the vision I had from Sonya Lee, he didn't appear to be that tall."

"So that leaves Luke," Zack concluded.

"Either that," Jenny added, "or it's someone we haven't considered yet."

Jenny let out a yawn as they left Shenanigans and headed toward Eddie's Brewery, which was just a few doors down. "It's only, like, nine-thirty, and I'm already beat," Jenny confessed. "I don't know how these kids do it."

"They're on a different schedule," Zack replied, "and they nap."

After showing their licenses to the bouncer, they went inside. This place was more like a sports bar, with televisions showing every game imaginable. Several giant vats sat behind the bar, indicating the beer was home brewed.

"Ooh," Zack said, "I just might have to try me one of these."

Jenny glanced at the few patrons that sat in various places throughout the room, her eyes landing on a blond man sitting alone at the bar. "You go right ahead," she said. "I'm going to have a nice conversation with Scott Sweigert."

Chapter 8

"Scott Sweigart?" Jenny asked as she sat next to the blond man at the bar.

His eyes were bloodshot and half closed; his head rested in his left hand, and his right hand held an empty glass. Looking up at Jenny—an act which appeared to take a lot of effort—he slurred, "Not again. Not here."

She smiled pleasantly, glancing down at his feet, guessing his shoe size to be eleven or twelve. "I'm not here to interrogate you."

"Then how do you know my name?"

"You probably wouldn't believe me if I told you."

"Try me. This whole month has been friggin unbelievable." He held up his empty glass to the bartender, who took the hint.

"Are you sure you should be having another one of those?" Jenny asked. "You look like you may have had enough."

"Am I still sitting here? Have I passed out yet? Do I still feel pain? As long as those answers are all *yes,* then I have *not* had enough."

Jenny understood what he meant, even though he hadn't said it right. "Fair enough. How do you plan to get home?"

He shook his head slowly, looking on the verge of tears. "I have no idea, and I don't care."

"You need to be able to get home," Jenny suggested.

"No, I don't." He was just about as drunk as anyone Jenny had ever seen. "I'll just sleep right here." He pointed clumsily to the ground. "On the floor."

"I don't think they're going to let you sleep on the floor."

"Who are you, anyway?" He asked as another drink appeared in front of him. He nodded his appreciation toward the bartender and then swayed to face Jenny.

"My name is Jenny; I'm a psychic."

He simply looked at her, as if he was trying unsuccessfully to focus.

"I saw a vision of you, talking with Sonya Lee behind the prescription counter at Jensen's. She was telling you that you needed to be more assertive and start asking girls out."

"I *did* ask a girl out. I asked *Lisa* out, and now she's dead." He suddenly looked confused, asking, "Hey, how did you know about what Sonya said to me?"

"I'm a psychic," Jenny repeated. "I saw it in a vision."

"A vision, huh?"

Zack took a seat next to Jenny at the bar, placing his home-brew in front of him.

"I told you that you wouldn't believe it," Jenny told Scott.

"I don't know what to believe anymore. No. I take that back. You know what I believe? I *believe* that if I had the balls to ask Lisa out sooner, she may have been hanging out at my place that night instead of at her place getting *killed*." Tears began to fall down his cheeks. "Oh, God, she's dead. And Sonya's dead." He downed his drink in one gulp and lowered his head to cry.

Jenny turned to the bartender. "I don't think he should be having any more of these."

"They're virgin," he replied. "Have been for a while. It's easier to do that than to refuse customers; sometimes they get ugly when you won't serve them."

"Good tactic. Is he paying for those?" Zack asked with a smirk.

"He's got a tab," the bartender explained as he dried some glasses. "I'm not adding these on. From what he's been telling me, he knew both Lisa Penne and Sonya Lee personally. He's taking it pretty hard. I can't say I blame him for getting wasted." He gestured in Scott's direction. "You able to get him home?"

"Me?" Jenny asked. "I don't think so. I don't even really know him."

"I'll be fine," Scott said, suddenly lifting his head, his defiant words blending together. "I'll walk home. Or I'll just sleep right here. I don't give a shit. It doesn't matter." He folded his arms on the bar, placing his forehead on top of them.

Jenny wondered if he had just passed out.

"He's in rough shape," Zack said.

The bartender nodded in agreement. "Uh-huh."

Jenny reached out her hand and patted Scott's back, noticing the lack of a burning sensation from the contact. A wave struck her instead. The dim lighting of the bar was replaced with the bright fluorescents of a classroom, but her hand was still on his back, and his head was still resting on his folded arms at his desk.

He raised his head with an expression of both sadness and humor on his face. "I studied so hard for this."

"A C is not the end of the world," she heard herself say. A feeling of warmth encompassed Jenny's body; she was in the presence of someone she was attracted to, and things seemed to be going in the right direction.

"But..." he replied, laughing despite his disappointment. "But it should have been an A. You got an A, and we studied together." He reached over and snatched a paper off of Jenny's desk, holding it up next to his own. "How did I get that wrong? I *knew* that one." He playfully slammed the papers down on his desk, announcing, "I am such an idiot."

"Don't worry; you'll still go on to sell drugs to people."

"Yeah," Scott retorted with a laugh, "on a street corner."

The vision faded when Scott raised his head, looking at Jenny with half-closed eyes. "I've got to hit the little boys' room," he told her.

He got off the bar stool, wobbling his way toward the restrooms.

Taking advantage of Scott's absence, Jenny turned to the bartender and asked, "What has he been saying about the murders? Anything particularly interesting?"

The bartender shrugged. "He's just upset that someone has been killing his friends...I really feel for the guy, to tell you the truth. I didn't even know those girls, aside from seeing them in here from time to time, and their deaths have affected me. I can't imagine how it would feel if I knew them both."

"That's just it," Jenny said, "he's one of the few people who actually did know them both. I'm wondering if he holds the key to this thing."

"Do you think he did it?" the bartender replied, appearing surprised.

Jenny looked squarely back at him and asked, "Do *you*?"

"That guy? I wouldn't think so. He seems more the pushover type, if you ask me."

She silently acknowledged that sometimes the *pushovers* get tired of that role and reach their breaking point. Although, based on the vision she'd just gotten, she didn't think that Lisa had been treating him badly. In fact, Lisa seemed more than happy to be talking with him. Had things gone sour between them, Jenny imagined she would have been subjected to an ugly vision instead of one that portrayed Scott as a likable guy.

Clearly, Lisa didn't think Scott Sweigert was the killer. Coupled with the fact that his feet were the wrong size, Jenny didn't either.

Scott returned from the bathroom, placing both hands clumsily on his bar stool. With great effort, he lifted himself up, trying to get seated in the tall chair.

"Here," Jenny said, "let me help you with that." She put her hands on his elbow, guiding him into place.

"Thanks," he said mechanically. He then looked up at Jenny, squinting, as if trying to focus on her face. Covering one of his eyes with his hand, he leaned in closer and said, "Who are you?"

"My name is Jenny," she said again. "I'm a psychic."

"A psychic?" He seemed to think about that for a while, but only added, "Huh."

"Is something wrong with your eye?"

"No," Scott replied, using his free hand to raise a finger. "Covering one eye helps me see only one of everything."

"Wow," Zack said from behind her, "he's toast."

"I think we should get you a ride home," Jenny suggested to Scott.

"I don't need a ride home," he replied. Leaning in closer to Jenny, he softly said, "Home is sad."

"Do you live by yourself?"

Without answering, he once again folded his arms over the bar and placed his head on them.

Jenny let out a sigh and dug into her purse. Pulling out some cash, she addressed the bartender. "When you see fit, can you use this money to call him a cab? There's enough for a tip for the driver if he can make sure he gets into his house okay. There's also a little something for you for your trouble." She waved a bill in the air before placing all the money on the bar.

"Sure thing."

"Do you know where he lives, by any chance?" Jenny asked. "Just in case he can't tell the driver his address?"

The bartender shrugged nonchalantly. "His license will say if he can't."

"Good point," Jenny replied. She patted Scott on the back and said, "You hang in there, okay buddy?"

He raised one hand in the air in a half-hearted wave before plopping it back down on the bar.

The bartender winked at Jenny. "I think I'll be calling sooner rather than later."

"Good idea." Jenny waited for Zack to finish his drink before they headed outside to go to the Tap House, which was only a few doors down from Eddie's Brewery.

Once outside, Zack remarked, "You seemed awfully concerned about him back there. Something tells me you don't think he's our guy."

"I don't," Jenny admitted.

"I noticed he had normal feet," Zack said.

"Yup. Normal feet and, according to the vision I got from Lisa, a pleasant personality."

"Didn't Sonya incriminate him in a vision?"

"Not necessarily," Jenny said. "She might have been trying to finger Jason Lewis, the guy with the sick wife and the nine-and-a-half-wides." She shook her head with frustration. "I can't help but think it's more random than what we're investigating."

"You say random," Zack noted, "but these killings seem awfully deliberate."

"I know. Random is the wrong word. I feel like they are more of a result of a chance encounter—like both girls happened to look at the wrong guy cross-eyed, and he didn't take to it too kindly."

"What makes you say that?"

"The fact that they're guessing," Jenny replied. "The girls are clearly offering up suggestions, but it's not like in previous cases where they've let me know with certainty who we're dealing with." She blew out a long breath. "If they knew they wronged someone, they would most likely remember that and make me aware of it. Since that's not happening, I imagine that they upset somebody without even realizing it."

"That's going to make this case harder to solve."

"I believe *nearly impossible* is the phrase you're looking for."

After an unenlightening trip to The Tap House, the couple headed to the car. Unlike when they had arrived, people crowded the streets, swarming in every direction, their loud voices permeating the night.

"I have to admit," Jenny began, "I'm looking forward to going to bed. This old lady is tired."

"I'm getting that way myself," Zack added. "That homebrew was good, but it's putting me to sleep."

The car wasn't that far from the Tap House, so they arrived quickly. "It looks like all four tires are intact," Zack noted. "That's a good thing."

Jenny froze. "Yeah, but this time we've got something else to worry about." She swallowed and added, "There's a note on our windshield."

Chapter 9

"What does it say?" Zack asked.

Jenny pulled her sleeve down over her hand so she wouldn't leave any fingerprints on the paper. Removing it from the windshield wiper, she flipped it over to see both sides. "It's just a smiley face," she said to Zack.

He looked up and down the street, saying, "It doesn't look like there are any notes on the other cars."

With the fatigue suddenly gone from her body, Jenny asked, "What should we do?"

He started examining the buildings, stating, "One of these places has to have a security camera. We can't possibly go oh-for-three."

"It's dark," Jenny replied. "Even if there is a camera, how clear would the picture be?"

"Maybe not super clear, but probably at least good enough to get an idea of the guy's build."

After giving him a moment to look around, Jenny asked, "Are you seeing any?"

"Not yet, but that doesn't mean they aren't there."

Jenny gave him a little more time before stating, "Don't we already have an idea of his build? It takes a big guy to have a size fourteen shoe."

"Skinny guys can have big feet," Zack replied.

"Do you think somebody may have seen him put the paper there? Maybe we don't need a camera—maybe we have an actual eyewitness."

"It's possible," Zack said as he seemed to give up his search for a camera. "The trouble is, even if somebody saw it, they may not have taken notice. Or if they did, they may not be able to remember it tomorrow. Drinks in bars are expensive, so I bet a lot of these kids get liquored up at home before they come out." He walked over and put his arm around Jenny's shoulder. "They might not make the most reliable witnesses."

"I guess I can tell Detective Brennan about this in the morning," Jenny said with defeat. "Although, it's possible that it's not even related. Could it be that some drunk kid just left a random friendly message and it happened to be on our car?"

"Yup. I doubt that's the case, though, considering he's messed with our car two other times today. But it's possible."

She leaned against the Honda, looking at the picture in her hand. "It was smart of him to leave this...if it was him. There are a million witnesses around, but even if someone questioned him about it, all he's doing is putting a smiley face on my car. That's hardly illegal. In fact, if you didn't know any better, it could be considered a friendly gesture."

"Agreed. He just wants us to know he's around and is watching us."

"It's effective," Jenny replied, warding off a chill, "and scary as hell."

"Well, if it makes you feel any better, we should be safe. We're staying on the second floor of a hotel. He can't sneak in through a window, and we can make sure he doesn't come in through the door."

"What if he's got a gun and he's waiting to pick us off in the hotel parking lot?"

"We'll run from the car in zig zags—make it harder for him to hit us," Zack said with a smirk, pulling Jenny in playfully for a hug. Kissing her on the top of her head, he said, "Let's just call it a night, shall we? We can go back to the hotel, lock the door and put all of this behind us for a while."

Nothing in the world sounded better to Jenny.

Jenny emerged from the shower in the morning to the announcement from Zack, "Your phone rang while you were in there. I didn't recognize the number."

Heading to her phone, Jenny saw she had a message. "Hi, Mrs. Larrabee, this is Aiden Fowler with Lab Co. I'm afraid the drug test you requested for John Zeigler came back positive for crack cocaine. If you have any questions, please feel free to give me a call." He left a number, and the message ended.

Jenny sat at the edge of the bed motionlessly for a moment. With all that had happened the day before, this whole episode had slipped her mind.

"What was that about?" Zack asked.

"John. He failed his drug test, which isn't surprising, but now I have to figure out how to confront him with this information. We made a deal that he would go back to rehab if one of his tests ever came back positive, but I never really thought about how I would make that happen if the time came." She looked down at her feet. "I guess I was always just optimistic it would never happen."

"Don't you think he knows he's going to fail it?"

"I would assume so...although, it had been a few days, apparently." Lifting her gaze to her husband, she asked, "How long does crack stay in your system?"

"You're asking me as if I know the answer," he replied with a smirk.

Jenny only giggled.

Zack pressed some buttons on his phone, saying, "How long had it been, exactly?"

Exhaling as she thought, Jenny said, "I think it was two or three days."

"It looks like it could be questionable as to whether or not he would fail it. More sensitive tests could detect the crack, but it might have flown under the radar if they used a basic test."

"You know I ask for the most sensitive tests."

"I know that," Zack said, looking up at her, "but he may not."

She sighed, lowering her shoulders. "Okay, so maybe he thought he could get away with it. How am I supposed to let him know he didn't?"

Zack sat next to Jenny on the bed. "This is just my opinion, but I think you should get his sister to gather up some buddies—or some of the rehab guys or something—to all show up at once and confront him. Enough people to convince him that putting up a fight would be a bad idea." He leaned into her with a little nudge. "You remember what happened the last time you tried to get him to agree to go to rehab?"

"He was a full-fledged addict then," Jenny said, "and that was an intervention."

"Still," Zack added, "if you didn't have some big guys guarding the doors, John would have been out of there."

Jenny didn't respond, silently contemplating what Zack was saying.

"Even with all of the guys there, he managed to tear up his house pretty bad. Remember that? It took me forever to fix that place up."

With a half-hearted smile, she said, "I hoped that once we got him out of that house, he'd leave that lifestyle behind."

"It's a strong pull, I'm sure," Zack replied. "He'll probably battle those demons forever. Sometimes it will get the best of him; other times he'll be able to beat it. With a good support network, though, he can hopefully spend most of his time clean."

"I guess you're right; thanks, hon." She patted Zack's leg. "I suppose I should give his sister a call—sooner rather than later, for more reasons than one. I want to get this over with."

"You've got this," he said, standing up. "If anyone can handle that phone call with all the necessary tact, it's you."

While she appreciated the support, for a fleeting moment she wished she was somebody else—somebody completely and utterly irresponsible, who nobody ever expected anything from. Those people never had to make phone calls like this. They could just skirt though life, acting selfishly, not even really disappointing anybody because no one expected anything more from them.

But people like that never changed the world.

With a reluctant sigh, Jenny made the call to John's sister, Amanda, who agreed to gather up her husband and his brothers for a second time. Although she seemed disappointed, Amanda was clearly grateful for the information. Jenny was relieved by that reaction, making her realize that she had done the right thing by making the call—even if it had been painful to do.

After hanging up the phone, she finished getting ready to head out to the park. "I hope our car is drivable," she noted as she gathered up her purse to leave.

"Well, I parked within sight of a security camera and next to a news van from Saint Louis; it was the safest place I could find."

"I think we should get a rental today and leave our car in the parking lot of the police station," she suggested. "Maybe we can find one with Missouri plates and blend in a little better."

"That, my darling wife, is a fabulous idea."

Much to Jenny's relief, they found their car intact in the parking lot, and it didn't explode when the key turned in the ignition. After a quick stop at a rental agency and a drop-off at the police station, Zack and Jenny drove off in a white Acura with in-state tags and headed for Buford Park.

The park was buzzing with morning joggers and dog walkers. Despite the open nature of the park, three different concrete walking paths cut through the grassy space, each with a wooden sign at the entrance marking a different length trail. "We should take this one," Jenny noted, pointing at a sign with a red square etched into the wood; it advertised a three-mile loop. "That's the path that at least one of the girls used to take."

"You don't know which girl?"

"Nope," she replied, "I only know which path."

Seeing a woman walk by pushing a stroller, an ache burned within Jenny. In an instant, she realized how desperately she missed her baby. As much as he drove her crazy sometimes, she didn't feel right without him. "I hope we can get this solved quickly and get back to Steve," she said as they started to walk the red trail. "I don't want to leave here until the killer is caught, but I'm dying to get home and squeeze my baby."

"I get that," he said, grinning at her sideways. "You just saw that woman with the stroller, didn't you?"

"Yeah," she confessed.

"I'm feeling the same way when I see people with dogs. I miss Steve more, obviously, but I do miss Baxter, too. He was our first baby, after all."

Jenny wasn't entirely convinced that Zack missed the baby more than the dog. His bond with the dog ran deeper than it did with his own son, a notion that had been plaguing Jenny since Steve had been born. Zack's parenting role had slowly been increasing, and Jenny's tolerance and love for the baby had exploded in recent months, so she had been more accepting of the imbalance. However, she did have a deep-rooted fear that Zack's relationship with Steve would never be quite what it should be.

"See, that dog even *looks* like Baxter," Zack said, pointing at a black lab mix. "I miss my buddy."

Jenny found herself getting irritated that he missed the dog more than the baby, so she simply changed the subject. "I'm going to try to concentrate a little bit...see if I can get a reading." After taking a few more steps, she added, "I do feel a little funny, actually, like someone's trying to get through to me."

"That's promising."

"It *is* promising," Jenny replied, "although I have no idea what I'm supposed to be focusing on. I just know there's something here that I should be paying attention to."

Once again, Jenny studied every male face that jogged by, feeling nervous, wondering each time if she was looking at the face of a killer. The supernatural buzz stirring inside her did nothing to help with her uneasiness. In her mind, every man was the culprit, and that left her feeling exposed and vulnerable.

Without warning, her eyes found their way to a dense patch of clovers to the right of the path. She immediately honed in on one in particular, plucking it with her thumb and forefinger, examining it closely.

Four leaves.

As she was trying to determine the significance of this latest development, Zack commented, "Good find."

She shook her head. "It wasn't a find. I was led to it."

"It means something?"

"It must," Jenny said, still trying to figure out the message.

"Maybe it's a good luck charm...an indication that we're about to find the killer."

"That would be spectacular," she said sincerely, tucking the clover into an outside pocket of her purse, "for more reasons than one."

They continued down the path, Jenny confessing, "I do feel awfully strange. Something is definitely up...I just wish I knew what it was."

"Well, keep your eyes open. Maybe you will see what you are meant to see."

A man jogged by in the opposite direction, making eye contact with Jenny, raising a hand and giving a slight smile in acknowledgement. Jenny wondered if she had just witnessed basic cordiality or if she was being taunted. A second man ran by with a nod, invoking the same fear. Another guy stood still and watched Jenny go by as his dog sniffed the base of a tree.

This was maddening.

With an upward glance, Jenny saw something off in the distance. Squinting, she asked Zack, "Is that a person?"

"Where?"

"Up ahead. To the right of the trail."

Zack searched around until his eyes landed on what Jenny wanted him to see. "It looks that way," he agreed. "It looks like he's just sitting there. Are you thinking what I'm thinking?"

"I'm thinking we may have just found our homeless man."

Chapter 10

Zack and Jenny walked closer to the man, who sat in the sun on a dirty blanket. He was dressed for chilly weather in tattered clothes, wearing socks on his hands. His long hair and matted beard suggested he had been out on the streets for a while.

This was the person Jenny had seen in her vision while visiting Lisa's apartment.

Unsure how to begin, Jenny simply said, "Hello, there. How are you today?"

He glanced up at her, squinting one eye in the bright sunlight. "Oh, you know," he replied. "Same old, same old."

Jenny guessed his age to be in his mid-forties; she wondered what his story was and what led him to be out there. For the moment, she didn't feel anything frightening, so she operated under the assumption that he was innocent until proven guilty.

"You doing okay?" she asked. "Do you need anything?"

"Breakfast," the man said plainly.

"You need breakfast?"

"It should be coming soon."

Jenny looked around in all directions, seeing only joggers and dog walkers. "Somebody brings you breakfast?"

"Jeremy does. Some days he's not real, but the breakfast is always real." He looked at Jenny. "A biscuit with sausage and eggs. That's what I like. One day he brought me a biscuit with *ham* and eggs. I didn't care for that too much, but I ate it. If the Good Lord is willing to provide me with food, who am I to argue?"

Jenny smiled at him, her curiosity about how this man ended up on the streets satisfied. "The man who brings you food isn't real sometimes?"

"Most days he isn't. Sometimes he is. It all depends."

Jenny decided to drop it. "What is your name, friend?"

"My name is Sir Walter James Southerland." He pulled the sock off his hand and held up three fingers. "The third." He wriggled the dirty sock back on.

"What should I call you?" Jenny asked.

"You should call me Sir Walter James Southerland the Third. That's my name." There was no hostility in his tone.

"Okay, Sir Walter James Southerland the Third...How long have you lived out here?"

"Oh, you know. A couple of days."

"Just a couple of days?"

"That's right."

Jenny glanced down at his feet. He was wearing two different shoes, both of them designed for the right foot. One shoe was substantially larger than the other, potentially as large as a size fourteen.

"Ah," he announced, "here comes my breakfast."

Jenny looked up, following the path of Sir Walter James Southerland the Third's eyes, seeing what appeared to be a college student heading toward them. The young man's smile was broad, and his hair was in long dreadlocks, pulled together behind his head with an elastic band. Indeed, he had two wrapped breakfast sandwiches in one hand and a gallon of water in the other.

Once the man got close enough, he looked at Zack and Jenny, announcing, "I didn't realize we'd have company this morning; otherwise I would have brought more food."

"Oh," Jenny said with a smile, "don't worry about us. We're fine."

After handing off the sandwich to Sir Walter James Southerland the Third and setting the gallon of water down on the ground, the young man stuck out his hand and introduced himself as Jeremy Washington. Zack and Jenny introduced themselves as well.

Turning to Sir Walter James Southerland the Third, Jeremy asked, "Why are you wearing socks on your hands?" He took a seat on the blanket, tucking his legs underneath him.

"That's how they wanted to be worn today."

"Oh, yeah?" Jeremy replied with a grin. "They told you that?"

"Yup. They sure did."

"So, what do you want to hear this morning?"

Sir Walter James Southerland the Third looked up at the sky and said, "How about a little something about encouragement?"

"Okay," Jeremy said, "encouragement." After thinking for a moment, he closed his eyes and bowed his head; the homeless man did the same. "So do not fear, for I am with you; do not be dismayed, for I am your God. I will strengthen you and help you; I will uphold you with my righteous right hand."

"That's a good one," Sir Walter James Southerland the Third said. "What was it?"

"Isaiah, forty-one ten," Jeremy told him. Both men unwrapped their sandwiches and started to eat.

Jenny watched this exchange with awe. "Do you two do this every morning?"

Jeremy nodded, tucking the bite of food into his cheek. "Yes, ma'am."

"How long have you been doing this?"

Jeremy looked over at his homeless friend, asking, "What's it been, about a year now?"

Sir Walter James Southerland the Third nodded, his eyebrows down, genuinely replying, "At least two or three days."

Fascinated by this, Jenny couldn't help but ask more questions. "How did it start?"

"Well, I'd seen him here a few times," Jeremy began, "and then one Sunday my pastor said something in his sermon that really struck me. He quoted John three-seventeen and three-eighteen. 'If anyone has material possessions and sees his brother in need but has no pity on him, how can the love of God be in him? Dear children, let us not love with words or tongue but with actions and in truth.' At that point I realized I had just walked by my brother, here, many times without offering a hand. That's not the behavior of a Christian."

Jenny stood frozen as she listened.

"So, one morning I brought him breakfast," Jeremy continued. "At first, I just handed it to him, but after talking to him a few times, I realized he's got some interesting things to say. Now I take a few minutes each morning to eat my breakfast with him."

"A biscuit with sausage and eggs," Sir Walter James Southerland the Third said.

"That's right," Jeremy replied with a smile directed toward his friend. "A biscuit with sausage and eggs." He returned his attention to Zack and Jenny. "I mix mine up from time to time, but his is always the same."

"And some scripture," Sir Walter James Southerland the Third added. "Can't forget about that."

"That's right. We always start with a little scripture. We always remember that we owe all our blessings to Him." Jeremy looked inquisitively at Zack and Jenny. "So, what brings you two here today?"

"Actually, I'd like to discuss that with you on your way out, if you don't mind," Jenny replied. "Perhaps a little more privately."

Jeremy's face remained pleasant, although it reflected curiosity. "Sure, we can do that." He turned back to Sir Walter James Southerland the Third and asked, "Isn't it a little hard to eat with socks on your hands?"

"It is, but it makes them happy."

"Well, that's very kind of you. How's your toothpaste supply? You running low yet?"

Reaching into a bag, the homeless man pulled out some toiletries. "Still have half a tube. I am running low on this, though." He held up a bottle of hand sanitizer.

"I can bring you more of that tomorrow. Anything else you need?"

"No, sir." He packed up his belongings. "I saw the doe again this morning."

"Oh, yeah?"

"I'm thinking she's with child."

Jeremy smiled. "That sounds about right. 'Tis the season."

"She isn't scared of me," Sir Walther James Southerland the Third announced proudly. "I think she's used to me by now."

"Well, you're harmless. She knows that."

"I'm not harmless if you're a biscuit with sausage and eggs." He took an exaggerated bite of his breakfast.

With a loud laugh, Jeremy said, "That is true."

After a short time, the men finished up their meals and Jeremy stood up. Sir Walter James Southerland the Third handed him an empty water jug, and, with a handshake, they agreed to meet in the same place the next morning.

As Jeremy, Zack and Jenny headed back toward the parking lot, Jenny felt a bizarre mixture of respect and inadequacy. She couldn't have revered Jeremy any more than she did, but she felt ashamed of herself for not having behaved similarly at that age. "Wow," she began, once they were out of earshot of the homeless man, "you really are an extraordinary person."

"Me? Nah," Jeremy replied. "I'm just doing what the bible tells me to do."

"Not everybody does that," she commented.

"It's not much," he said sheepishly. "It's a breakfast sandwich and a jug of water. I feel like I should be doing more."

"Well, if every person of privilege reached out to one disadvantaged person the way you have, we wouldn't have any disadvantaged people."

"He still wouldn't have a home," Jeremy replied sadly.

Jenny knew in her mind that was only temporary. Once this ordeal was over, Sir Walter James Southerland the Third would be housed somewhere. Whether that would be a mental facility or a jail cell remained to be seen. "Well, I'd like to ask you a few questions about him, if you don't mind."

"I don't know how much I'll be able to answer, but you can certainly ask."

"You say you've known him for about a year..."

"That's right."

"What's his story? Do you know?"

"Not really. Honestly, I'm not even sure he knows his own story at this point. As you could probably gather, he's got some mental issues."

"Yeah, I figured that," Jenny replied. "I just didn't know if you were able to talk to him before things got this bad."

Jeremy shook his head. "Things were this bad when I met him."

"Is he ever violent at all? Or paranoid? Does he ever talk about people being out to get him?"

"No," he said, "he talks about conversations he's had with bugs and stuff like that, but he isn't hateful at all."

"What about drugs or alcohol?" Jenny asked. "I noticed he was out of hand sanitizer, and some people have been known to drink that stuff for the alcohol content."

"He calls alcohol *the devil's drink;* he apparently doesn't touch the stuff. I got him that hand sanitizer about a month ago; I think he just ran out of it."

"No drugs, either?"

"Nah." Jeremy let out a laugh. "He has conversations with bugs as it is...like, two-way discussions. He doesn't need drugs."

After a few steps in silence, Jenny treated her next statement as if it were unrelated. "Hey, do you happen to know about those killings in town?"

"I know they've been happening, but I don't have any information, if that's what you mean." He glanced at her out of the corner of his eye. "Do you mind if I ask who you are?"

Jenny smiled guiltily, realizing it was time to come clean. "My name is Jenny—I'm a psychic who is working on the murder investigations. One of the victims showed me an image of Sir Walter James Southerland the Third; he must have spooked her while she was on the jogging trail one day. I came out here to see if he was dangerous at all."

"You're a *psychic?*"

"Believe it or not, yes."

"And you had a vision of Sir Walter James Southerland the Third?"

"Yes."

"That's amazing," Jeremy replied. "That's truly amazing."

Jenny hoped he'd be able to get beyond that and answer her question.

Fortunately, he did. "Well, I can see why Sir Walter James Southerland the Third would scare some females joggers—especially the ones who are by themselves. He does look pretty unkempt. But I can assure you, he's harmless. He's a good man—a man of God—he just has mental issues."

They were reaching the parking lot, so Jenny squeezed in one last question. "Jeremy, let me ask you this...If I am able to get Sir Walter James Southerland the Third into a facility, would you still bring him breakfast?"

Jeremy froze, looking at Jenny. "Why do you ask? You think you can get him into a facility?"

"Probably."

"But..." Jeremy began, "but you just met him."

Jenny only shrugged. "It doesn't matter; he clearly needs a hand. But I'd hate to see your little ritual end just because he found some shelter. I'm sure your visits make his day."

Jeremy continued to look dumbfounded. "Yeah, I would still visit him. Man, I'd love to see him with a roof over his head. You can really arrange that?"

Jenny smiled. "I can try. I just hope he'd be willing to go...not every homeless person wants to be housed. Maybe you can help convince him."

"I'll definitely do that."

"Great," Jenny said. "I'll start making some phone calls."

Looking as if he was battling tears, Jeremy added, "If you can make that happen, I'll be so happy. Thank you. Truly." He reached in and gave her a hug. "God bless you."

"God bless *you*, Jeremy," Jenny said sincerely. "You are an amazing young man to do what you've been doing."

After modestly shrugging off Jenny's compliment, Jeremy bid goodbye to the couple and headed toward his car. At that point, Zack turned to Jenny and remarked, "Are you really going to get him into a facility?"

"I'm going to try." They walked in the direction of their rental car.

"I hate to burst your bubble," Zack said, "but you might be offering to help a man who is guilty of two murders. Did you see the size of one of his shoes?"

"I did," Jenny replied as she opened the door and climbed in. "But I look at it this way—if he's innocent, then I'm helping him find a home. If he's guilty..." She made eye contact with her husband. "Then I'm putting him into a supervised situation where he can't strike again."

"Very smart thinking," Zack replied as he buckled his seatbelt. "Well played."

"I have to admit, I don't think he did it," Jenny added.

"So far, you don't think anybody did it."

She frowned. "I know. I guess I shouldn't jump to those conclusions. I have to remember what one of the detectives from the meeting said—that the killer is probably an ordinary guy...someone you could have a conversation with and not know you were dealing with a murderer."

"That's scary," Zack noted.

"It is scary," she replied as she backed out of her parking space. "And do you know what pisses me off?"

"Uh-oh."

"No, it's nothing bad. It's just that you've got a guy like Jeremy Washington, who takes time out of his day every morning to have breakfast with a homeless man, and he gets zero recognition. Then you've got a friggin psycho who kills two innocent people, and he's all over the news. What is that about?" she demanded. "What message does that send to the young people out there who are looking for their fifteen minutes of fame?" She shook her head. "It's totally backwards. We sensationalize the wrong things. It's like we're *encouraging* people to become serial killers."

"No argument here."

She let out a frustrated sigh. "It makes me mad."

Her phone rang from inside her purse; Zack pulled it out and handed it to her. She didn't look at the caller before she answered, fearful she would miss the call. "Hello?"

"Jenny. Detective Brennan. I need you to drop whatever you're doing and get to 4363 Warren Road in Kensington…we've got another victim."

Chapter 11

After a twenty-five minute drive, Zack and Jenny arrived at the address Detective Brennan had given them. Unlike the other cases, this house was in the suburbs, situated on a normally quiet residential street. At this moment, however, the scene was chaotic, with reporters and neighbors swarming around the yellow tape that surrounded the yard.

This time, Jenny called Detective Brennan from the safety of her car, and the tiny detective made her way through the crowd to meet them. Preferring to stay anonymous inside her vehicle as long as possible, Jenny simply rolled down the window when she arrived.

"Thanks for coming out," Detective Brennan said. "They're still processing the scene, so it will be a little while before you can go in there."

"That's fine," Jenny replied. "What happened this time? More of the same?"

"The M.O. was the same…cut screen, head trauma, slit throat, no other apparent reason for being there besides the murder. The victim is different, though. This one's name is Rachel Ann Moore. Twenty-four, Caucasian, hairdresser, has no affiliation with Perdion College that we know of, and obviously lives outside of town." She glanced back at the scene before adding, "She had two roommates—that were home at the time of the attack. Neither heard anything; they just found her like this in the morning."

"That's so scary," Jenny muttered.

Detective Brennan shook her head. "It appears our perp wanted this one and this one only."

"Well, I received another little message from my friend last night. There was a piece of paper with a smiley-face on it on my windshield. We're hoping that a security camera may have gotten a glimpse of the person who put it on there—which may be the same person who did this."

"Could be," the detective replied. "Or it may not be. You got the paper?"

"It's at the hotel. I didn't realize I'd be coming out to see you this morning."

"Yeah," she replied with a snort, "neither did I."

"If you want," Jenny began, "I can try to look into the note for you. I realize you probably can't spare any manpower to investigate something that may be totally unrelated."

"That'd be great," Detective Brennan said. "If you find anything out, let me know. I've got to get back to the scene. I'll come get you when they're ready for you. In the meantime, would you be willing to talk to the roommates? Right now they're inconsolable, but once they're able to speak more coherently, maybe you can get some information from them that will spark something. So far, they haven't been able to give us any facts. They claim they didn't hear or see anything unusual until they found Rachel this morning."

"Sure, I can do that."

"Okay. I'll let you know when they get it together enough to talk." The detective patted the door of the car and walked away without saying goodbye.

Jenny sucked in a deep breath as she closed the window. Turning to her husband, she asked, "So, what do you make of this?"

"It sucks," he replied, "but it just may be different enough that we can narrow down the one thing these women have in common. She said the victim wasn't affiliated with Perdion...that should eliminate a pretty big segment of the suspect pool. Okay, let's review." Zack leaned back in his seat, unbuckling his seatbelt. "The first guy we suspected was Luke Thomas."

"I never suspected Luke Thomas."

"You haven't suspected anybody."

"True," Jenny replied.

"Well, Luke certainly had the opportunity to kill Sonya, being her upstairs neighbor and all. He may have seen Lisa out at one of the bars or in the gym. And his feet are most likely big enough to leave that size fourteen print outside the window."

"How would this latest victim fit in?"

"Maybe she cuts his hair? Maybe she was in one of the bars?"

Jenny said nothing as she nodded, thinking about his words.

"Next," Zack continued, "we had that Jason guy with the sick wife."

"Small feet," Jenny said.

"Small feet," he repeated. "He was a regular customer at the pharmacy and the diner. Also a haircut customer, you think?"

"I'm sure the detectives will get a complete list of Rachel's clients. They already know his name; they'll notice if it comes up."

"What about that hammered guy from the bar last night?"

"Scott? Do you really think he'd be capable of killing someone as drunk as he was? He could hardly even stand up. I bet he went home and went straight to bed."

"We may want to double-check with the bartender and the cab driver to make sure he went directly home. His drinks were virgin after a while; it's possible that he sobered up before the night was over."

Jenny grunted as she squinted. "His feet weren't all that big, though, either. I really have trouble believing that it's him."

"I guess we can eliminate the homeless guy from the park," Zack added. "I don't think he'd have the means to get all the way out here."

"You're probably right." She let out a sigh. "I have to make some phone calls about him. Please don't let me forget that with all that's going on here."

"I'll try. No guarantees."

"Great."

"What about that four leaf clover?" Zack asked. "What do you think that means?"

After thinking for a moment, Jenny came up empty. "I don't know. I wish I did. I thought it meant we were close to finding the killer, but it doesn't look that way."

Jenny's phone, which was still on her lap, began to ring; John Zeigler's name appeared on the screen. Dread filled Jenny's body. "Hello?"

"Jenny." His tone sounded both irritated and urgent. "It's John. My sister is here telling me I need to go back to rehab."

Hanging her head, Jenny replied, "Yes, I'm afraid that's true."

"I had one moment of weakness. I don't plan to do it again. I appreciate your concern, but I really don't need to go back to rehab."

Jenny spoke with less conviction than she would have hoped. "That was part of our arrangement."

"I'm telling you, I don't need it. I'm fine. I'm not going to go back to my old ways."

"We had a deal," Jenny said softly. "You signed a contract."

He sighed impatiently on the other end of the phone. "You're not seriously planning to make me do this."

Doubt ravaged Jenny's mind. She had no idea if she was doing the right thing or not. However, she stood firm. "I'm sorry, John."

"I don't have to go, you know. This is America. You can't force me to go."

"You're right," she said slowly. "I can't. But I also don't have to provide you with a house and a job..."

"I can move back in with my sister," he replied defiantly.

Jenny heard a female voice in the background.

"Fine," he said. "Then I'll just make it on my own." A beep signaled he'd hung up.

Feeling the urge to cry, Jenny let the phone drop into her lap. She closed her eyes and remained motionless for several moments. "This day sucks," she eventually said.

"I take it Amanda's conversation with John isn't going that well."

"No, apparently not."

"Did you expect it to?"

Jenny didn't reply. She only rubbed her temples, thinking to herself that she was tired of hearing that her expectations were unrealistic.

"You remember how it went last time," Zack continued. "He tore his house apart before he agreed to get help."

Jenny's eyes remained closed. This was a rental property—in her name. She hoped he wouldn't resort to destruction this time.

"It'll be fine," Zack added. "He'll eventually cave, he'll get some help and then he'll be calling you to thank you."

She opened one eye and looked at him. "And *that* isn't an unrealistic expectation?"

"Let's assume for the time being it isn't."

She rested her head back, focusing on the roof of her car. "Today, I really wish I wasn't me."

Jenny's phone chirped with a text message from Detective Brennan. *One of the roommates is ready to talk now.*

Turning to Zack, she remarked, "I guess that's my cue. I think the roommates are most likely on the other side of the tape, so I'll have to go it alone. No offense, but they probably won't let you come with me."

"Well, you know where to find me," Zack replied as he pulled out his phone.

Brushing her hair into her face, Jenny left the car and walked with her head down as she neared the crime scene tape. Just at the edge of the cordoned off area, Jenny found Detective Brennan with a young woman in flannel pants and a hoodie, her hair in a messy ponytail. The woman seemed positively distraught; Jenny could only assume she was the roommate.

Detective Brennan lifted the tape, allowing Jenny to duck under. Despite her efforts to remain anonymous, Jenny found herself surrounded by flash bulbs in every direction. For a brief moment, she feared the crazy guy would find her again.

She quickly determined that her troubles paled in comparison to the young woman in front of her, who had just lost her roommate. Jenny reached out her hand and placed it on the girl's trembling shoulder. "I'm so sorry for your loss."

The woman, who appeared to be in her mid-twenties, nodded wordlessly; her tear-soaked cheeks and puffy eyes spoke on her behalf.

Upon touching the woman, Jenny heard a distinct voice in her head. With a sympathetic tone, Jenny asked, "If I say 'All for all and one for one,' would that mean anything to you?"

The woman's look of anguish immediately turned into dismay. "How do you know that?"

"I just heard Rachel say it." Jenny smiled compassionately at the roommate. "I can hear messages from the deceased; that's why I'm here."

The young woman appeared to go numb, as if overwhelmed by too many emotions at once.

"My name is Jenny Larrabee; I've been trying to figure out who has been doing this by listening to the victims. Unfortunately, none of the girls know who the killer is so far, so they haven't been able to tell me much. I'm hoping to be able to get a little more from Rachel once I get inside."

The woman nodded; Jenny was under the impression she wouldn't remember any of this later.

In a flash, an unbearable pain ravaged Jenny's head and another tore through her throat. She grabbed her neck, trying to understand what was happening.

Then she heard the voice.

Chapter 12

In an instant, the sensation was gone. Jenny turned to Detective Brennan with wide eyes and said, "I'd like to speak with you privately." Keeping her intense stare fixed on the detective, she added, "Now."

Detective Brennan called on another officer to come over and console Rachel's roommate before escorting Jenny to a more secluded part of the lawn. "What happened to you back there?" the detective asked with concern.

"I felt the attack," Jenny replied breathlessly. "I saw it and felt it and heard it." She took a moment to gather her bearings, trying to determine the best way to tell the story without getting hysterical. "I felt this pain…this horrible, agonizing pain in my head, and then my throat. I was confused…panicked. I wasn't sure what was going on—whether I was dreaming or awake. I put my hand to my neck and felt the blood spurting. I struggled to breathe. I wanted to scream, but I couldn't make a sound. And then I heard it."

"Heard what?"

"A man's voice. In little more than a whisper, he said, 'To drink to excess is the devil's work. May God accept you and keep you, despite your sins.'" Jenny shook her head. "I may not be saying it quite right, but it was something to that effect."

"The killer said that?" the detective asked.

Jenny nodded. "Rachel heard it before she died."

"So you're saying this is *religiously* motivated?"

"Apparently," Jenny replied with a shudder. "The crazy part is, I know that voice." She closed her eyes and held up her hand. "I mean, *Rachel* knows that voice."

"Who is it?" Detective Brennan asked eagerly.

"That's just it," Jenny confessed. "She can't place it. It's familiar, but she doesn't know whose voice it is." She looked helplessly at the detective. "I get the feeling it's one of those tip-of-her-tongue kind of things."

"The chief is going to want to know this," the detective said, mostly to herself. Focusing on Jenny, she added, "Stay here. I'll be right back."

She watched Detective Brennan walk away, realizing she was by herself in that area of the yard. She felt exposed—like a sitting duck. The person who had been harassing her could very well have been in that crowd, watching her. On one hand, she wanted to look around to see who was there, but at the same time, she didn't. Using only her eyes, she quickly surveyed the faces surrounding the crime scene tape, deciding none of them looked familiar or particularly menacing.

Nonetheless, she was relieved when Detective Brennan came back with the chief. He stuck out his hand, which Jenny shook, as he said, "Thanks again for coming out here. I hear you may have something?"

"I do," Jenny said, recounting her story to the chief.

He nodded as he stroked his chin. "You haven't been in the house, correct?"

"Correct."

"Tell me...what side was she lying on? Rachel, I mean."

Jenny thought briefly before saying, "Her left. She reached up and grabbed her neck with her right hand, and the guy spoke into her right ear."

He looked at her for a long time, their eyes locked in what appeared to be a visual standoff. Jenny wasn't exactly sure what was going through his mind, so she continued to stare at him curiously, waiting for him to say something.

"You don't know whose voice it was?" he eventually asked.

"It was familiar," Jenny said. "Rachel knew it from somewhere; that's the best I can say."

"If you heard it again, would you recognize it?"

"I'd like to think so," she replied, "but I don't want to promise anything."

He turned to Detective Brennan, saying, "Sonya and Lisa were not avid church goers; we know about this one, yet?"

"I can ask the roommates," Detective Brennan said. "They're just now becoming calm enough to start talking."

The wheels in the chief's head were obviously turning. "I don't think church is how he knew them. According to Jenny, the guy didn't like how much these girls drank. If he only saw them in church, how would he know that they were partiers?" He shook his head. "No, I'm thinking we have a guy who has witnessed these women at their drunkest. In order for him to be offended by their drinking, he must have seen it happen first hand."

"The bars then, sir?" Detective Brennan asked.

The chief nodded. "It may be the only connection between Rachel and the two other victims. She didn't go to Perdion; she didn't live near the others. Find out where she liked to go when she drank." He turned to Jenny. "Are you willing to do me a favor?"

"Absolutely."

"I'm assuming this latest victim hung out on Center Street, just like the others. Can I count on you to go to the bars tonight and strike up conversations with every man you see? I mean, literally, every man you see? Maybe one of the voices will sound familiar."

Jenny laughed nervously. "I can do that." She decided to leave off the part about that being ridiculously weird. "I should also note that I have been...harassed...lately, by somebody who keeps messing with my car."

"You've been *harassed*?" the chief asked with dismay. His tone became protective. "What do you mean you've been harassed?"

With a sigh, Jenny admitted, "The most recent episode happened last night when I was parked on Center Street—somebody put a smiley-face note under my windshield wiper. That, alone, wouldn't have been a problem, but this was just the latest incident. Earlier in the day, someone messed with my rearview mirror and slit my tires in two separate episodes."

"That's not good," the chief declared.

"I know. I was going to see if any local businesses have security cameras that may have caught him putting the note on my car. If it's the same guy who is doing this," Jenny pointed to the house, "maybe that can give us an idea of what he looks like."

"Definitely look into the cameras. Tell the businesses that I, personally, want you to have access to the surveillance videos. If any of the businesses give you trouble, tell them to call the station to verify. I would have one of my guys do it, but I can't spare the personnel."

"Understandable," Jenny said.

He turned to Detective Brennan. "Go back and talk to the roommates; see what you can find about Rachel's acquaintances in the bars and if she went to church. Ask about her customers at the salon, too—see if any of them seem like possible candidates."

"Sure thing, sir." The determined detective headed back to the roommates.

"So, I can count on you to scour the bars tonight?" he asked Jenny.

"I will do that." It looked like the conversation with the chief was about to end; Jenny couldn't help but ask the question that had been burning in the back of her mind throughout the entire visit. "Chief? Before you go...Can I ask you something?"

"Sure."

"Why do you take me so seriously? I mean, you should...I am a legitimate psychic." She softened her tone. "But why do you believe in me so much?"

Once again, he looked at her intently—expressionlessly, at first, but then a smirk graced his lips. "I'll tell you when I have a little more time."

He turned and walked back into the house.

Jenny caught up with Detective Brennan and Rachel's roommate, who was introduced as Lauren. The other roommate, Bella, had joined them as well, finally able to gather enough composure to speak. The women stood arm in arm, leaning on each other for support, both visibly trembling.

"I know this is hard," Detective Brennan said to the roommates, "but the more you can tell me, the more likely we are to catch the guy who did this."

The women nodded, closing their eyes and sniffing, holding wadded up tissues in their hands.

"What can you tell me about Rachel's social life?" Detective Brennan asked. "Where did she like to hang out?"

"She goes into town quite a bit," Lauren said as she wiped her eyes.

Jenny noticed the use of present tense; that one little word made her incredibly sad. Clearly, the impact of what had happened that morning hadn't fully sunk in yet.

Lauren continued, "She also likes Damon's down on Oak Street."

"When she went into town, where did she go?" the detective asked.

"Center Street."

"Any particular bar her favorite?"

"Depends on her mood." Bella rested her head on Lauren's shoulder; Lauren, in turn, squeezed her a little tighter.

"Did you ever go into the city with her?"

"Sometimes."

"Did she drink a lot when she went out?"

The look on Lauren's face implied that the detective should read between the lines. "She has a good time."

"How would she get home when she drank at Center Street? It's a pretty long drive from there."

"Sometimes we would drive her," Bella said.

"What about the other times?"

The women remained quiet.

"Did she drive herself?" Detective Brennan asked.

With a reluctant nod, Lauren softly replied, "Yeah."

"Do you know of any men she may have interacted with while she was at these bars?"

The roommates looked like they were doing their best to think, but they were coming up blank. Eventually, Bella shook her head and admitted, "I don't know. There are people, definitely, but I can't give you any names right now. I can't even think straight." Tears once again worked their way to the surface.

"I know it's difficult," Detective Brennan said, "but it will really help us a lot if you can give us some names."

Lauren closed her eyes tightly, as if that action would help her think better. "There was this guy, Reggie..."

"It wasn't Reggie," Jenny heard herself say.

The roommates and Detective Brennan all looked at Jenny, who sheepishly replied, "Rachel would have recognized Reggie's voice."

"Who is Reggie?" the detective asked.

"He's this guy she's been seeing," Lauren explained. "They met at Shenanigans."

"Were they serious?"

"They've been out a few times. I wouldn't call it serious."

An image flashed in Jenny's mind. A man with a closely-cut beard and a baseball cap appeared; his tight shirt highlighted his muscles and the barbed tattoo on his left arm. They sat at a bar, which Jenny recognized to be the long serving table from Shenanigans. "You want another?" The man asked. The vision fizzled out just as quickly as it came.

"Reggie had an accent," Jenny said. "New York, I think."

The roommates looked at her with awe. "He was from Brooklyn," Bella confirmed with a nod.

"The killer doesn't have an accent," Jenny replied with a confident shake of her head. "It wasn't him."

"Any other names you can give me?" Detective Brennan asked, notepad in hand, ready to write.

The girls rattled off a few more names, but they were only first names, and they were common. None of them triggered any type of memory with Jenny as the name Reggie had.

Soon, a terrible shriek echoed from the crowd, causing Jenny and the roommates to look in that direction. A hysterical woman tore through the crowd, shoving people out of the way as she worked her way to the crime scene tape. Lauren and Bella seemed to recognize her and ran toward her, arms outstretched, ultimately ending in a three-person hug from opposite sides of the yellow barrier.

Jenny hung her head; it was all she could do to keep from crying.

"Well, at least I got some names," Detective Brennan said.

"Can you take a picture of that list and send it to me?" Jenny asked, straightening her posture—she had to remember there was work to be done. "That will help me when I go to the bars tonight."

"Consider it done," the detective replied.

Jenny glanced back at the house—a small, nice ranch that looked so innocent, like it was once an ideal place to live. Now it was forever marred. It would always be referred to as *that house*. "Do you know what happened there?" people would ask their friends, from this day forward. "The woman who lived there was killed in her sleep."

Jenny shook her head rapidly, trying to rid herself of the thought. "How long do you think it will be before I'm allowed in there?" she asked the detective.

"Not sure. They're processing for evidence—it could be a while."

Looking over at the three women who were still in a tragic embrace, Jenny decided she couldn't take it anymore. "I think I'm going to head into town and see if I can get my hands on any surveillance tapes. It'll be more useful than waiting out here."

Detective Brennan snapped a picture of the list on her phone, pressing a few buttons with her thumb. Without looking up, she said, "Let me know if you find anything worthwhile. I just sent you the names."

"Okay," Jenny agreed. "Will you tell me once it's safe for me to go in the house?"

She lifted her eyes to meet Jenny. "You'll be the first to know."

Chapter 13

The urge to cry was nearly overwhelming as Jenny got into the car and closed the door behind her. She didn't say a word when she turned the key and pulled out of her parking spot.

"You okay?" Zack asked.

She responded only with a slight nod, fearful that opening her mouth to speak would invoke a flood of tears.

She was grateful when Zack said no more about it and allowed her a moment to gain her composure. After a few miles had gone by, she decided she was strong enough to disclose some basic facts. "Her name was Rachel Ann Moore. She was a twenty-four year old hairdresser with two roommates."

"Roommates, huh? That's a new one."

A brief flash of the two crying women entered her mind, but she forced it away. Getting emotional only would have slowed her down. "They were home when it happened, too," she said mechanically.

She recounted the full story to Zack, ending with the chief's conclusion that the bars would be a better place to look for the killer than churches. Zack didn't reply immediately, apparently mulling over everything she had just said. "So, we're dealing with a guy who is against alcohol," he eventually said. "He's not against *murder*, apparently, but alcohol is a no-no."

"Go figure," Jenny replied.

"And the chief thinks you'll find this guy in a bar? If he hates the idea of drinking, the only reason he'd be there would be to find women to kill."

"Correction...women to *save*," Jenny replied, "at least in his mind."

"Either way, we're looking for a sober guy in a college bar," he replied. Glancing at her out of the corner of his eye, he added, "That shouldn't be too hard to spot, especially by the end of the night. Any guy who isn't trashed should stick out like a sore thumb."

Jenny didn't reply.

"You know who this pretty much eliminates as a suspect?" Zack continued.

"Scott Sweigert?"

"Exactly. If the killer is against drinking, then Scott isn't our guy."

"What if he's only against *women* drinking?" Jenny posed. "Maybe it's a gender thing."

"I suppose it could be," Zack admitted. "I guess I shouldn't dismiss him so soon. But this does kind of point us to a couple of people you might not like to consider as suspects."

Jenny lowered her eyebrows as she drove.

"Luke Thomas, for one," he went on.

"Luke?"

"Remember, we talked about the fact that he might not drink because he was an athlete. Maybe it goes beyond that."

Shaking her head, Jenny said, "You'll be able to knock me over with a feather if it's him."

"Don't close your mind to the possibility. I know he and Sonya were friends, and she doesn't think he was capable of it, but people have betrayed their friends before. It could be that he just acted like he liked her, but deep down inside he was disgusted by her drinking."

"Then why did he rearrange the furniture and put the bat under the couch?"

"It sure makes him look innocent, doesn't it?"

Jenny sighed, realizing she'd been outdone.

"The other person we may want to consider is Jeremy Washington."

117

"What? That guy who brought Sir Walter James whatever-his-name-was the food? You're out of your mind."

"What was his reasoning behind bringing him breakfast?" Zack asked.

"It's what the scripture says he should do...but nowhere in the scripture does it say you should kill people who drink too much."

"I'm sure it condones excessive drinking somewhere in the bible."

"And it also condones murder," Jenny replied. "*Thou shalt not drink* is not a commandment; *thou shalt not kill* is."

"Well, it appears that this person is concerned about God accepting and keeping the victims, despite their sins. Apparently, he views drinking to be more offensive than murder."

"This is all just so bizarre," Jenny said, shaking her head. "I have always associated religion with good deeds...not this."

"I have to admit, I know very little about the subject. Is there any religion anywhere that preaches that it's okay to kill someone who lives an unholy lifestyle?"

"I'd like to think not," she replied, "but there may be some kind of backwoods cult out there saying that very thing."

Jenny's phone rang, and she reached for the button on her steering wheel to answer it. "Oh," she said with a laugh, "this isn't my car."

Zack fished in her purse for the phone, handing it to her. She answered, hearing that Mick was on the other end. "Hey, Jenny," he said solemnly.

"Uh-oh," she replied.

"Yeah, things here aren't going that well."

"What's happening?"

"John's locked himself in his bedroom. He tried to leave, but we wouldn't let him, so he barricaded himself in his room."

"Maybe he just needs some time to cool down," Jenny proposed. "The ambush tactic has its advantages, but it obviously has some flaws, too."

"Hopefully he'll cool down," Mick replied, "but that was pretty ugly."

"It was ugly the first time, too. He tore his house apart. What did he do this time?"

"Nothing like that. He's just really, really angry, and he's saying that he'd rather move out and live on the streets than go to rehab again." Mick made a scoffing sound. "It's obvious he's never lived on the streets before."

"But you have," Jenny said encouragingly, "and maybe you can use that to your advantage." She heard her GPS interrupt the conversation, spitting directions into her ear, but soon she was able to continue. "Once he's had a little time to process this, maybe you can have a nice, calm conversation with him and let him know that rehab is a better alternative than the streets."

"I can try," Mick replied with a skeptical groan. "The problem is that he keeps insisting that he doesn't need rehab. He says he agreed to go last time because he was an addict, but this time he isn't. He just had one slip-up, and rehab isn't necessary."

Jenny let out a sigh; this was the one thing she wasn't sure about. "Maybe he's right, and it isn't necessary. To be honest, I have no idea if it is needed or not…but let's leave that decision to the professionals. If they say he doesn't need to go back to residential care, then fine. Maybe he can just attend some outpatient meetings or something." Jenny softened her tone. "Hopefully, if you take that approach, John will be willing to at least talk to rehab folks. Then we can work on a plan based on what they say."

Mick's voice reflected resolve. "I'll do that. I will give him a little more time first, though. I don't think he's quite ready for reasonable conversation yet."

After a little more discussion, they ended the call, and Jenny dropped the phone back into her purse.

"I guess things aren't going so well?" Zack asked.

"Not so much."

"Well, hopefully we'll have better luck with the cameras."

"I hope so," she muttered. "I don't think I can handle any more bad news today."

Shenanigans looked only slightly less crowded than it had the night before, but Jenny found the stale beer smell to be even stronger. "If I was pregnant and walked into this place, I think it would make me puke," she told Zack in a hushed tone as they entered.

"I'm not sure this is a popular hangout for pregnant people."

The couple walked toward the bar, where a different bartender than the night before busied himself with cleaning and stocking. "Hey," he said as they approached. "What can I get for you?"

"I don't suppose you have coffee?" Jenny asked.

"Sure don't."

"Then I'll take a diet soda."

Zack ordered a soda as well—with full calories—and then Jenny began to speak as she sat on a stool. "We're actually here for a reason. We're wondering if you have a security camera that would capture images from across the street. I parked there last night, and something happened to my car. I'm hoping it may have been caught on tape."

"You'll need to speak to the owner," the bartender replied, placing two sodas in front of them. "He's in the back; I can get him for you."

"Thanks," Jenny replied, throwing a ten dollar bill on the counter.

"You want to get lunch?" Zack asked. "The nachos were pretty good last night."

"Really? I wouldn't have expected that. This doesn't exactly look like the type of place that would have good food."

"That's often the case. Sometimes the best food comes from little hole-in-the-wall places where somebody's grandma is in the kitchen."

"Cooking with love?" Jenny asked with a smirk.

"Exactly. Those nachos had a lot of love in them; you could taste it."

The bartender emerged from around the corner, followed by a dark-haired man dressed in a black shirt with the Shenanigans logo, which seemed to be the required uniform for all of the bar's employees. He greeted Zack and Jenny with a big smile, saying, "Hello. My name is Oliver Jacoby. What can I do for you today?" He had an accent, which Jenny couldn't determine to be English or Australian, but it didn't matter. She loved it, no matter where it was from.

"Hi," she began, "we were wondering if you have any security cameras that would capture images from across the street. I parked there last night, and somebody messed with my car. I was hoping to get a glimpse of who it was."

"I'm terribly sorry," he replied. "We do have security cameras, both inside and out. Let me see what I can find out for you. Do you have an approximate time frame I should be looking at?"

She turned to Zack. "We got here, what, about eight? And got to the car around ten-thirty?"

"Sounds about right," Zack said.

"What kind of car do you drive? And where was it parked?"

Jenny explained exactly where the car had been, giving him the make and model. "What you'll find is someone putting a note on the windshield."

He raised an eyebrow. "A note? Was it a threatening note?"

"Yes. Very." While that was a bit of an exaggeration, it may have held an element of truth to it. Besides, he may not have agreed to look at the video if he knew it was only a smiley face.

"Alright," the owner said, "let me get on that straight away. I'll come back out and get you if I see anything." He disappeared back in the direction he came.

"Did you hear that?" Jenny asked Zack like a giddy schoolgirl. "He's going to get on that *straight away*." She mimicked his accent, swooning involuntarily.

"Should I feel threatened?" Zack asked with a smile.

"Maybe," she confessed, "although, I don't want to sleep with him. I just want him to come home with us and talk to me all day long."

"Just talk?" Zack looked at her skeptically.

"I guess he could clean the house while he was there, if he wanted to feel useful." For a brief moment, Jenny envisioned Oliver pushing a mop across her kitchen floor, casually telling stories in his beautiful accent while she sat at the table eating doughnuts with her feet up. She had to force that thought out of her head, though, before she got too excited about it.

After sipping her soda through her straw, she added, "Why don't you order up a plate of nachos for us, and I'll go outside and take a look at the front of the building—see where the cameras are located. Maybe that will give us an indication of whether or not we should hold out any hope."

"Sounds like a plan," he replied.

She got off the stool and walked out the door, looking up into the sun at the building's façade. At first, she scanned for cameras along the roofline and under the awning, but something drew her attention to the bar's name on the bricks. Three-dimensional green letters spelled out the name Shenanigans.

A four-leaf clover dotted the i.

Chapter 14

"I think this place holds the key," Jenny said excitedly when she returned to her chair.

"Good camera angle?" Zack asked.

She shook her head. "The four-leaf clover...I'm pretty sure I know what it means." She explained her finding, adding, "I got this feeling over me when I saw it out there, like someone was taking satisfaction that I finally got the hint. And, you know, I thought about it...Rachel was already dead when I found the clover. She's probably the one who led me to it."

"What makes you say that?"

"She's the only one who has even the slightest clue about the killer's identity. She heard his voice, and it's familiar to her. Although she doesn't know exactly whose voice it is, I believe she's under the impression that he's related to Shenanigans somehow."

Zack frowned as he considered the idea. "Sounds plausible. Now, we just need to figure out who the voice belongs to."

Jenny tipped her glass toward him like a toast. "At least now we know where we can narrow our focus."

After the nachos had been eaten, Oliver came back out and approached the couple, placing one hand on each of their backs. "I think I've found something for you," he said in his beautiful accent. "It isn't the clearest image in the world, but it's better than nothing, I suppose. If you follow me to my office, I can show you."

Jenny eagerly walked in the back, hopeful that she—or Rachel—would be able to recognize the man who had left the note. While she realized he would most likely appear as a mere shadow considering it was night time, she was guardedly optimistic that the person's mannerisms would be clear enough to be recognizable.

Oliver's office was small and horribly disorganized, dashing Jenny's fleeting dream of him one day cleaning her house. "Excuse the mess," he said with a chuckle. "I wasn't expecting visitors."

"It's okay," Jenny said. "I'm just grateful that you can show us something."

He sat in the chair in front of a monitor, using a mouse to click the fuzzy, black-and-white movie into motion. "If you look," he said with a point, "you can see the man come up and stop at your car."

Jenny squinted, trying to get a better view of the grainy image in front of her. The man appeared to be somewhat stocky, not necessarily tall, and wearing a baseball hat tucked low over his head. Aside from that, none of his features were discernable in the low-budget video.

"Huh," Jenny said, a bit disappointed. "Can I see it again?"

"You can see it as many times as you'd like," Oliver replied. He clicked and dragged, causing the man in the video to walk quickly backwards away from the car. When he released the mouse, the scene played out again at regular speed. "Want me to pause it?" he asked.

"Please." He stopped the video at the spot where the man was at the windshield. Stepping even closer, Jenny practically put her face against the monitor. Unfortunately, nothing struck her about the person she was looking at; both she and Rachel were coming up blank.

"Is there any way I can get a copy of this video to the police?"

Oliver looked curious. "It's really a police matter? The note was that bad?"

"It may be related to the women who have been turning up dead around here."

His eyes grew wide. "You mean that could be the man who's been doing it?" He pointed toward the video.

"It's possible."

"Just outside my bar?"

Jenny didn't want to disclose that she suspected the man was a regular *inside* the bar. She responded with a simple nod.

"They found another victim this morning, you know, "Oliver continued, "out in Kensington."

"Yeah," she replied, "we were there this morning."

He looked at her with awe, apparently realizing her involvement in the case was more than he'd anticipated. He also seemed to comprehend the potential importance of that video. "I will figure out a way to get this to the police," he said emphatically. "I won't do anything else until I do."

Jenny smiled graciously. "Thank you. Hopefully, with a little help from your surveillance tape, the victim in Kensington will be the last."

"What do you say?" Zack asked as the couple approached Rachel's house, where Jenny had been officially granted permission to go inside. "You think our note-leaving friend could have had a size fourteen shoe?"

"I couldn't see his feet in the video," she replied.

"He wasn't all that tall. Stocky, but not tall. I wouldn't think that—a—he'd be able to fit through a window, and—b—he'd have shoes that big."

Jenny tried to envision the windows the killer had used for entry; they were relatively high. Would that stocky man from the video have been able to pull that off? "It depends on what constitutes his stockiness," she concluded. "Were there muscles under those clothes, or just too many potato chips? If he was a short, body-builder type, he may have been strong enough to climb through the windows."

"Or maybe it's not the same guy."

"I can't imagine this isn't the guy," Jenny replied. "Why on earth would somebody just randomly target my car if it wasn't related to the case?"

"I didn't say it wasn't *related*," Zack said. "I just suggested it might be a different person leaving the notes."

She glanced at him as she pulled up to the house. "You think there are two people involved in this?"

Zack shrugged. "I'm just looking at the facts. We have a nimble guy climbing through windows to kill these women, and we have a stocky guy leaving notes on the car. Either the nimble guy is stocky, or the stocky guy is nimble, if you prefer to look at it that way...or else we have two different people."

"The only thing scarier than the thought of one lunatic running around killing women is *two* lunatics on the loose."

"There are more loonies than that out there, I assure you," Zack replied. "They're just not directly involved with this case."

Jenny stopped the car and put it in park. "I could have done without that little nugget of wisdom," she said.

She got out and walked through the crowd, which was smaller now than it had been before. Lifting the crime scene tape, she ducked under and continued with determination, finding Detective Brennan standing near the front steps. The detective was holding a coffee, which Jenny assumed was once again a substitute for sleep.

"Glad you could come back," Detective Brennan said, swirling the cup in her hand. "You ready to go inside?"

Jenny took a long, hard look at the front door; it looked intimidating. Despite the fact that she wasn't really sure if she wanted to see what was inside, she replied, "Yeah, I'm ready."

After putting covers over her shoes, Jenny walked in through the front door. Detective Brennan followed, saying, "Rachel's bedroom is..."

"Don't tell me," Jenny interrupted, holding up her hand. Realizing she'd been rude, she looked back and added, "Sorry. I just want my information to come from Rachel, if that's okay."

The detective bowed her head and held up her free hand, signaling she was willing to do this Jenny's way.

Focusing her attention back on the house, Jenny felt overcome by familiarity. She drank in the sight of the living room furniture—something Rachel had taken for granted but would never see with her own eyes again. The nostalgia of it all was nearly overwhelming.

Memories flooded Jenny's mind in a giant wave. Closing her eyes, she saw Lauren and Bella appear on the couch, dressed as if they were ready to go out for the evening. Bella had a beer and Lauren sipped from a large glass of water; Jenny had a full shot glass in her hand.

"Do you think he'll be there tonight?" Jenny heard herself ask.

"He's there every night," Bella replied, taking a drink from her beer.

Jenny felt a tingle brewing inside her at the thought of seeing him.

"You haven't given up on that yet? He's awfully young." Lauren noted.

"*No,* I have not given up on that...and I won't until I get what I want. I'm not looking to marry the guy, I just want my turn with him," Jenny clarified with a sly smile. "Last week he was flirting with me, I swear it."

"How do you even remember?" Bella asked, her words slightly slurred from the alcohol. "You were totally wasted by ten o'clock."

"Oh, I remember. I wouldn't forget that."

"How would you even kiss him?" Bella asked with a look of confusion. "He's, like, ten feet tall. You'd need a ladder just to be at eye level with the guy."

"I would make it work, believe me."

"Well, I don't know about you girls, but I'm ready to get out of here," Bella said, downing the last of her beer.

"Yeah, me too," Jenny replied. "Just give me a sec." She held up her shot glass. "To the three musketeers...all for all and one for one."

"You're hammered already," Lauren noted, "and we haven't even left the house yet."

Jenny shrugged. "Whatever." She tilted her head back and let the shot slide down her throat.

The roommates faded from view, and Jenny opened her eyes. While she was fairly confident that Rachel had been talking about Luke Thomas, she didn't want to disclose her discovery just yet. She wanted to see what else the house had in store before she explained any of her findings.

Instinctively, she knew which way to go to Rachel's bedroom, although she took her time getting there. She looked at each wall hanging, appreciating them more than Rachel ever had in her lifetime. Somehow, Rachel had assumed she would always be able to look at them; had she known her time was so limited, maybe she would have looked at everything just a little bit harder.

Entering the bedroom, Jenny was taken aback by what she saw. Blood. Everywhere. On the bed. On the walls. On the nightstand. On the lamp. On the book she had been reading. It was a library book; Rachel was supposed to return it.

Jenny instinctively placed her hand on her neck, fully aware that was where all of this blood had come from. Sadness engulfed her. Rachel had been too young to die. Lauren and Bella should have never seen this. The whole incident was just so tragic on many different levels.

The person responsible for this needed to be put away.

Jenny took two steps into the room, and the whisper of a voice echoed between her ears. *To drink to excess is the devil's work. May God accept you and keep you, despite your sins.*

She closed her eyes, focusing, trying to recall exactly where she'd heard that voice before. It was so familiar, yet she simply couldn't place it.

The devil's work.

The wheels in Jenny's brain turned frantically.

May God accept you and keep you.

Think. Think. Think.

Despite your sins.

Jenny clenched both fists and held them to her temples. No matter how hard she tried, she couldn't determine whose voice that was. She pounded her fists into her head, hoping that would help, but it only made her grunt with frustration when she still came up empty.

In another sudden image, Jenny lay on the bed, grasping her neck, feeling the blood spurt between her fingers. Her killer leaned over her, whispering his chilling words into her ear.

He was close to her.

She understood.

The vision left Jenny's mind in a flash. She looked over her shoulder at Detective Brennan, stating with wide eyes, "She got him."

"She got him? What do you mean *she got him?*"

"She bled on him. She marked him." Jenny couldn't hide the excitement from her voice when she added, "The killer may not be leaving his DNA at the scene, but she left hers on his clothes. If you find the guy, you'll definitely be able to connect him back to this crime." She looked back at the blood-soaked bedroom. "Now, we just have to find him."

Chapter 15

Jenny gripped the wheel as she spoke to Zack in the passenger seat. "I told Detective Brennan that I think Rachel may have had a thing for Luke Thomas, although I can't be sure that was who she was talking about. Her roommates made the comments that he was younger, he was *always there* and that he was incredibly tall. I remember that Luke frequented Shenanigans often, and that's the place we're focusing on." She shook her head, squinting, unable to rid herself of the feeling that Luke was an innocent man. "I realize he probably doesn't drink while he's there, being an athlete and all, and I guess it's possible he's also religiously opposed to alcohol. But I don't know. I'm just not buying that he's our guy. I got the distinct impression from Sonya that he's too harmless, and I can't get past that."

"Do you think Rachel was trying to implicate him in the vision?"

"I can't figure that out. At the end of it, I saw how that whole 'all for all and one for one' misquote happened, which is the message she had for her roommates when I first got there this morning. Maybe she just thought it was funny and she wanted Lauren and Bella to always remember it? Maybe she wanted me to know she had a crush on Luke so I could tell him that? Or maybe she was trying to point him out as a suspect." She let out a frustrated sigh. "I just don't know."

"Maybe you'll get an indication tonight when we go to Shenanigans."

"I hope so," Jenny said. "This cryptic stuff is too hard for me to figure out."

"Well, I was productive while you were in there, if that makes you feel any better."

"Oh, yeah? What did you do?"

"I did a little research into residential facilities around here, and I found a place called White Oak Psychiatric. It looks like they would provide good care for our friend, Sir Walter James Southerland the Third."

With all that had been going on, Jenny had almost forgotten about her promise. "That's fantastic," she said sincerely. "Do they make house calls?"

"What are you talking about?"

"I mean, will they go out and get him? Or do we have to arrange for him to come in?"

"Uh," Zack replied, "I haven't called them yet. I have no idea how this works. I can call them now, though...we have a little time to kill before we get back to the hotel."

"That sounds great." Jenny felt relieved at the notion of something being handled without her having to be the one to take care of it. Between this killer, John's relapse and now Sir Walter James Southerland the Third, she was feeling overwhelmed.

After a long phone call, Zack filled Jenny in on the details. "He'd need to come in voluntarily, since none of us are legally in any position to have him committed. They'd do an evaluation on him to see what he needs, and if they decide that residential treatment is appropriate, we can arrange that—if he's willing, of course." He tossed around some figures, letting Jenny know what the cost would be. While it wasn't cheap, they could easily afford it thanks to the inheritance she'd received from Elanor.

Elanor. Jenny still missed that woman dearly.

She pulled her car into a parking space at the hotel as she said, "Depending on how things go tonight, maybe we can head back out to Buford Park tomorrow morning. I'm not sure what time Jeremy comes with breakfast, but if we get there early enough, we can hopefully catch him. That way, we can have Jeremy's help when we try to convince Sir Walter to go to the facility."

"Sir Walter. You're on a first name basis with him now?"

They got out of the car and walked toward the hotel. "His name is too long and takes too much effort. I don't have that much energy right now."

"I like how he made himself a knight," Zack said. "The *sir* part of it is a nice touch."

Jenny laughed as they passed through the sliding glass doors. She waved to the desk worker as she told Zack, "I think I need a nap before we go out tonight; it might be a late one. I want to call and check on the baby, see how Mick is doing and then I am going to call it quits for a few hours."

"Sounds like a plan," he said.

The elevator ride was quiet, and Jenny felt herself growing more tired by the second. Bed was going to feel fantastic.

The doors opened, and Jenny fished around her purse for the room key while they walked down the hall. "What's that?" Zack asked.

"What's what?" Jenny looked up and saw a piece of paper wedged between the handle and the sill of their door. Glancing around quickly, she didn't see anything similar on the other rooms. Suddenly, her fatigue was gone and her heart was racing.

Upon closer inspection, the paper was a sheet of loose leaf with ragged edges, indicating it had been ripped out of a spiral notebook. "Don't touch it," she said. "Not with your fingertips, anyway. Don't get any of your prints on it."

Zack took several pictures of the paper before using his shirt as a buffer between his hands and the sheet. He removed the page and unfolded it to reveal the same smiley face they had seen the night before on the windshield.

"My God," Jenny whispered. "He knows where we're staying."

Security was at the door in a matter of minutes. "I just want to make sure nobody is in here before we go in," Jenny told them. "Somebody has been leaving little notes and messages for us everywhere we go. We're essentially being stalked, and I don't know what this person is capable of."

"I'm so sorry about this," the hotel manager said, her auburn hair pulled back into a small, tight ponytail. "The safety of our guests is my number one concern; I never want any of our guests to be uncomfortable."

Jenny couldn't help but feel like the manager was trying to avoid a lawsuit, or maybe a bad review. "It's not your fault," she said, "and I don't necessarily feel unsafe. Once we get in the room, I can use the deadbolt and the chain to make sure no one can get in. I just want to make sure there's nobody already in there waiting to ambush us."

"That's understandable. And whenever you need entry, please feel free to have security escort you to your room," the manager added. "We will gladly do a sweep for you before you go in."

The security man opened the door, instructing the others to wait outside while he looked around. After a few tense moments, he returned, declaring, "The room looks empty, but you can come on in and check it out for yourselves, if you'd like."

"I think I'm going to take you up on that," Jenny said, walking in and doing her own surveillance with the security guard still there. "I'll feel better if I see it with my own eyes." She, too, found nothing out of the ordinary. Apparently, the only thing this person had done was leave a note on the door.

"We can put you in a different room," the manager suggested. "Perhaps that will make you more comfortable."

Jenny shook her head helplessly. "I don't think that will matter. I imagine he'd just find our new room anyway. He seems to know every move we make, somehow."

"Do you have surveillance cameras?" Zack asked. "Maybe we can get a good look at the person who did this."

"We do in the lobby," the security man explained. "Unfortunately, we don't have cameras in the halls, so this is going to make things a lot more difficult. Lots of people come and go through those front doors throughout the day. Can you give me an approximate timeframe so we can narrow down the search?"

"We've been gone a good part of the day," Jenny said. "I'm afraid the window you'd be looking at is a few hours long."

He shook his head and grunted. "It's going to be tough, then. You may have to watch the video yourselves to see if anyone looks familiar."

Jenny thought about watching several hours' worth of people coming and going out of the lobby—she simply didn't have time for that. "I've seen the guy's silhouette before, on another surveillance tape—he's probably about average height and has a stocky build. Is it possible for you to look for guys fitting that description who come and go pretty quickly? Then maybe I can take a look." She put her hand on her forehead. "I'm in town working on the murder cases, and I have a long night ahead of me."

The man's eyes grew wide. "You think this is related to those murders in town?"

"It's possible."

The manager and security guard exchanged glances. "I'll get on that right away," he said excitedly. "If I can take part in bringing that guy down, I'd love it."

Bringing that guy down. Jenny imagined this hotel security guard had few opportunities to actually bring somebody down. Perhaps this would prove to be an extraordinarily exciting day for him.

Jenny thanked the staff for their willingness to help and then went into the room. With the adrenaline surge subsiding, fatigue was creeping back into her bones. She wanted to be able to go straight to bed, but she had a few matters to take care of first. After a quick pump-and-dump, she put on her pajamas and picked up her phone, dialing her mother. A million emotions hit her all at once when she heard her little son cooing in the background when her mother picked up. "Hi, sweetie," Isabelle said.

"Hi, Ma. I hear my baby. How's he doing?"

"He's okay. He's been a little fussy—he had a big night last night. He cut his first tooth."

Putting her hand over her mouth, she felt tears sting her eyes. "He did? He cut a tooth? Oh my gosh, I can't believe I wasn't there."

"There will be plenty more where that came from," Isabelle assured her.

"But not the first one."

"Well, you will learn that with teeth come fevers and fussiness. When he starts cutting his molars, you'll be wishing you were alone with Zack in a hotel."

The conversation continued for a few minutes; when Jenny hung up, she filled Zack in on the latest, her shoulders hanging low and her eyes sad. "I can't believe I missed the baby's first tooth."

"He'll never know," Zack replied. "Or care."

"I care." She found herself irritated by her husband's blatant lack of concern.

Zack glanced up at her. "Who was there when you got your first tooth?"

He had a point, but she didn't want to hear it. "Maybe I'm being dramatic, but I hate that I'm away from him. He's only going to be five months old for thirty days, and I've been gone for three of them. That's ten percent."

"You're torturing yourself."

"Do you know how quickly kids change at that age? We may go back to a totally different kid than the one we left."

"Isn't this the same kid that you feel the need to get away from sometimes? Just enjoy the break. Besides, a murder investigation is no place for a baby."

Jenny closed her mouth, realizing that complaining to her husband wasn't going to change the situation, but her mind still reeled. She wasn't sure if she was upset with Zack's nonchalant attitude or jealous of it. Either way, she ached for her baby, even though she knew, at times, he drove her crazy.

Again, she marveled over how conflicted she felt about parenting.

Conflicted. Suddenly, John popped into her head, reminding her of the other phone call she needed to make. She paused a moment, contemplating hopping into the bed and putting the covers over her head and pretending none of this was happening, but she knew she couldn't hide from what was going on. It was time for the big-girl panties, although she desperately wanted to keep them in the drawer.

Actually, at this particular moment, she wished she didn't own a pair.

With a sigh and the touch of a button, she dialed Mick. "Hello?"

"Hi, Mick. It's Jenny. How's it going down there?"

"Better," he replied, removing about fifty pounds from Jenny's shoulders.

"That's fabulous. What happened?"

"Well, after I let John cool down a while, I went into his room and talked to him. I didn't talk *at* him, like it must have seemed we were doing at first. He told me he slipped up and made a bad decision, but it wasn't like he was defending himself this time. He was admitting it. He'd had a bad day—a couple of contractors gave him the run-around, and he felt like he'd disappointed his client. He was feeling really down, and he thought getting high would help him get through it. He did it with the mindset of *just this once,* but you and I both know that 'just once' can get a person into a lot of trouble."

Jenny listened intently, hoping this conversation would continue to go in a good direction.

"I told him that we weren't trying to imprison him or punish him by making him go to rehab, but we wanted to make sure he found other ways to deal with bad days instead of turning to crack. I used your approach, telling him that he just needed to talk to the rehab people, and residential care might not be necessary. I let him know we were all there because we were concerned about him, and we weren't going to let him sink as far as he had been before."

Jenny released a breath. "I'm so happy to hear this."

"I also mentioned that he was just the first of us to screw up—that I would inevitably end up taking a drink sometime, and I needed him to kick me in the ass when I did...just like I was doing for him."

"So, did he ultimately agree to go to rehab?"

"He did. I'll be bringing him there later today."

Hanging her head, Jenny felt immense relief. "You don't know how happy this makes me."

"Actually, I think I do. Thanks for putting this into motion. I'm not sure I would have ever told you if you hadn't called. I would have felt like I was ratting him out, but now I see he needed the ass whooping."

"Just remember this when it's your ass than needs to get whooped."

After a little more small talk, Jenny hung up the phone, turned off the ringer and slid under the covers. Unfortunately, she felt a little more awake than she had before the phone conversations. Thoughts of someone lingering just outside her door kept her on edge, although she knew he couldn't get in through the security measures the room had. Just that fact that he knew so much about where they were was disconcerting. How was he getting all of his information?

Stop, Jenny silently instructed herself. *The best way to catch this guy is to get a good nap and hit Shenanigans tonight.* In order to calm herself down, she envisioned baby Steve cuddled up next to her, sleeping, his baby breath blowing softly against her cheek. Her anxiety suddenly melted away, and she was able to drift off within a reasonable amount of time—but not before she heard Zack snoring from the chair.

Chapter 16

Jenny admittedly felt nervous as they approached Shenanigans. The prospect of finding the killer was scary enough in and of itself, but her task of striking up a conversation with every male in the bar was a different kind of terrifying. She'd never been a flirt, or even overly-social for that matter. What on earth was she going to talk about over and over again with each guy she saw?

She parallel parked in the same vicinity as the last time, knowing it was well within the sight of the security camera. She patted the roof of the car as she got out, wishing it luck as it sat out there unattended, and she headed toward the bar with Zack by her side.

The same bouncer as before sat on a stool on the sidewalk, one foot propped on the chair leg and one on the ground. He sat cockeyed as a result, looking a little funny, but he seemed to recognize the couple, greeting them with a smile.

Remembering the drill, Jenny fished her license out of her purse. "I know," she said to him with a grin, "I need to show ID even though I'm old."

"I never said you were old," he replied, taking her license and giving it a glance.

That voice, she thought. *Oh my God, that's the voice.* Rachel screamed inside of Jenny, feeling as if she was physically bouncing around underneath her skin. Jenny began to tremble as the man studied her license, which stated in no uncertain terms precisely where she lived. House number. Street name. Apartment number. He didn't need to stalk his victims or follow them home—the women willingly showed their killer exactly where they could be found.

It suddenly occurred to her that the bouncer had made a comment, but, in her panic, she had no idea what had just been said. Was it something she should have responded to? "I'm addicted to the nachos here," she blurted, feeling the need to say something—anything. "We had to come back so we could have another plate tonight."

"They are good, aren't they?" he asked calmly, his tone indicating he didn't notice any changes in Jenny's demeanor. He gave Jenny back her license and took Zack's.

"Sure are," she replied as naturally as possible.

"Hey," he added as he examined Zack's identification, "are you having any luck on those murder cases?"

"Nope," she replied, perhaps a little too cheerfully. "None at all, unfortunately."

The bouncer handed back Zack's license and said, "That's a shame. I hope you can catch the guy soon."

"So do I," Jenny said with a quick glance down at his large feet, "but so far we've gotten nowhere."

Mercifully, Zack said nothing about narrowing their search down to this particular bar. Once they got the bouncer's approval to go inside, Zack simply walked in behind Jenny, grabbing her by the elbow once the door had closed behind them. "What was that about?" he asked. "You were acting funny."

She hoped Zack noticed that only because he knew her so well, and the bouncer didn't share a similar opinion. "It's him, Zack. The bouncer."

"What?"

"The bouncer. He's the killer. Rachel recognized his voice when he spoke to me. And it makes perfect sense...he sees their addresses when he cards them, and he's only been targeting older women, not the kids in the dorms. His victims have probably legally changed their addresses. And he's already awake in the middle of the night—it's not like he has to get up and go to work in the morning. In fact, he may have killed Rachel on his way *home* from work last night."

"You have to call Detective Brennan about this," Zack replied. "Now."

Without saying another word, Jenny pulled her phone out of her purse. Looking at the screen, she noticed she had both a missed call and a text from the detective already. At first, she wondered how she could have missed those, but then she realized she'd never turned her ringer on from her nap. Pressing the button to bring up the text, her jaw dropped when she read the words:

Call me ASAP. We've had a confession.

Jenny's head immediately began to spin. How could they have had a confession when the killer was standing just outside the door? "Zack," she said, "look at this." She held out her phone for him to see.

After taking a second to read the words, Zack raised his wide eyes to meet Jenny's. "Don't take this the wrong way, but are you sure the bouncer is the right guy?"

"Rachel is pretty darn sure," she replied emphatically. Her mind went back to a conversation she'd had with Kyle, her favorite private investigator, where he'd explained the notion of false confessions. "They have the wrong guy," she declared. "They have to."

"What are you going to do about this?" Zack asked.

"Text her back," Jenny said, her fingers already tapping the screen. "I don't want to call her in case somebody overhears."

Are you sure you have the right person? Rachel Moore just let me know it was the bouncer at Shenanigans.

She waited for a response, but there wasn't an immediate one. Muttering a few swear words under her breath, Jenny thought about what she should do next. "Come on," she said to Zack, motioning for him to follow her.

They approached the bar, where Jenny felt obligated to order nachos after her bizarre proclamation to the bouncer. After making that request, she said to the bartender, "Can I ask you a question?"

"Sure," he replied as he typed their order into a computer. "What's up?"

"The bouncer," Jenny said. "He looks familiar to me. Is his name Neal, by any chance?"

"Neal? No," he replied. "It's Mark."

"Mark..."she repeated. "What's his last name?"

"Neighbors."

Jenny wanted to make sure she had heard him correctly. "Like, the person next door?"

"*People* next door," the bartender clarified. "It's plural."

Trying to act nonchalant, Jenny simply said, "Huh. I guess I don't know him, then."

"He's not from around here," the bartender went on. "He just moved here a few months ago."

Jenny immediately began to wonder how many women had met a similar fate in the town where Mark Neighbors used to live.

Her phone, which was now on vibrate, came alive with a call from Detective Brennan. Jenny wished she could take it, but she didn't want to say anything out loud in front of the bartender. After the buzzing stopped, she typed, *please text me. I can't talk now.*

After what seemed like an eternity, she was made aware of a new voicemail. She determined she could listen—she just couldn't speak—so she punched in her code and put the phone to her ear.

"Hey," Detective Brennan's voice began, "I'm not sure what you got from Rachel, but this guy here has some details about the case that he just shouldn't know. We keep some things private so that we can tell which confessions are real, and he knows things about the crime scenes that he wouldn't know unless he'd been there. We're thinking his confession is legit. Maybe you can come to the station and see what Rachel and the others have to say about him. Hopefully, they'll be in agreement that we have the right guy. Okay, I guess that's it. Call me when you can. Bye."

Jenny looked at the phone when the message was over; Detective Brennan hadn't disclosed who the person was. Although the bartender had disappeared into the back, Jenny still didn't want to make any calls. She was unsure how long he'd be out of earshot. Brimming with curiosity, Jenny used a text to ask exactly who this self-proclaimed killer was.

A long moment passed before she saw *Gary Kimbrough* appear on her screen.

"Gary Kimbrough?" she whispered to herself. "Who on earth is Gary Kimbrough?" She held out her phone for her husband to see. "This, apparently, is the person."

Looking confused, Zack asked, "Who is that?"

"Exactly," Jenny replied, irritated. "It's like he came out of nowhere." She sighed and added, "Well, at least I have two names now. I guess it's better than none." Her fingers got busy on her phone, typing out a text to Kyle. *If you are there, please please please text me back asap.*

Her phone quickly shook in her hand. *I'm here.*

She closed her eyes for a moment as she silently acknowledged how much she adored Kyle. *I have two names for you...Mark Neighbors and Gary Kimbrough. Both currently live in or around Bennett, Missouri. Mark works at Shenanigans bar and is new in town. One of they may be killing women. Please find out as much as you can about them as soon humanly possible. Focus on religion—this might be a cleanse killing. Perp strikes at night. Don't want another victim tonight.*

A short pause. *I'm on it.*

The simple fact that Kyle was working the case made Jenny feel immeasurably better. If anyone could find the facts on these people, it was him. However, if Mark Neighbors was intending to slit another throat tonight, perhaps even Kyle wouldn't have had the time to stop him.

"The bouncer isn't stocky." Zack's words interrupted Jenny's thoughts.

"What?"

"The bouncer. He doesn't look like the guy in the video."

Zack was right; Mark Neighbors was tall and somewhat lean. She wondered what this mystery man Gary Kimbrough looked like. "Is it possible the two are friends?" Jenny asked. "Could it be that they are in this together, and Gary finally cracked?"

"We'll probably find out tonight, if the cops come and arrest Mark."

Jenny saw the bartender returning, so she placed her hand on Zack's arm to get him to stop talking. A plate of nachos appeared in front of the couple, along with two plates and some wrapped silverware. Jenny thanked the man and then looked at the unappetizing dish in front of her; she didn't really want this—she was still feeling heavy from the nachos she'd had earlier in the day.

"I hope you're hungry," she said to Zack, sliding the plate in his direction.

"Always." He readily dug into the mound of chips; this was his third serving in two days. She stifled a wince.

Keeping her voice soft enough for the busy bartender not to hear, Jenny remarked, "It's also possible that Mark asked someone to put the note on my car on his behalf—some drunk guy, maybe, who was coming into the bar. It wasn't like it was a threatening note or anything. It was a smiley face. The person who put it on there may have thought it was a nice gesture. And our car was right across the street from where Mark was sitting. It would have been easy for him to arrange that."

"There are lots of possibilities," Zack replied as he put a loaded chip into his mouth. Chewing it a few times and tucking it into his cheek, he added, "Our goal, however, is simple. We need to make sure this guy doesn't strike again, and if the police believe that they already have the right guy in custody, that responsibility is going to fall on us. They're not going to be out tailing this guy if they think the killer is already in a jail cell."

"We need to follow him home," she agreed, "and keep an eye on him all night. But I've been invited to go to the station and check out Gary for myself. I'd like to do that, just to figure out how this guy fits into this whole thing, but I obviously can't be in both places at once."

"I can follow Mark, if you want to call a cab to go to the police station."

"I'm not sure I want you tailing him in the middle of the night by yourself," Jenny replied.

"He's not going to do anything to me," Zack noted. "I'm not his type."

"I realize that...but if he recognizes that you're following him, he might have a problem with that. He's a big guy; how are you going to protect yourself if he decides to come after you?"

"I can use the gun your mother wanted us to get."

"Hush. I'm serious."

"I'll be in a car, with the windows up and doors locked. Besides, what benefit will I have if you're with me? Are you suggesting you'd be able to beat the guy up if he proves to be too strong for me?" He placed a huge nacho in his mouth and chomped exaggeratedly, as if to add an exclamation point.

"I am *suggesting* we use brains, not brawn, you big, fat pain in the butt." Jenny once again typed a message to Kyle. *If you can only find one thing out tonight, please tell me where Mark Neighbors lives.*

"What are you doing?" Zack asked.

"Finding out Mark's address. That way, we can see how close or far he lives. Then, depending on how populated or desolate that area is, we can devise a plan for following him home. If he lives out in the middle of nowhere, he'll definitely notice us driving behind him. If he only lives a few blocks away, we can probably get away with tailing him unnoticed."

"What if he's in between?"

"Then, we figure out something that will work." Jenny reached over to the plate, grabbed a chip and emphatically bit into it—just as Zack had done—while looking him square in the eye.

He couldn't help but smile. "Okay, you win that one. But what about the other guy? The confessor? Are you going to talk to him?"

"Maybe tomorrow," Jenny said. "The way I see it, he's in police custody, so he isn't a threat to anyone. That is, if he was a threat to anyone to begin with. He might just be some guy who is trying to get attention."

"That's a very strange way to do it."

"Well, clearly, helping the homeless won't get your face on TV. You've got to be a murderer before the news will devote any airtime to you." Bitterness was obvious in Jenny's voice.

Her phone buzzed once again. She checked the screen, seeing, *Mark Neighbors. 621A Hazel Drive, Bennett MO.* A smile splayed across her face as she looked at Zack and asked, "Can you call up a map?"

"It's not that far from here," Jenny noted, looking at Zack's screen. "A three-minute drive, tops. We can easily get away with following him home."

"We'd need to know what kind of car he has." Zack said. "We have to find it so we can make sure we are in a good position to watch him drive away."

Jenny lowered her eyebrows, wondering how that little detail had escaped her. Without saying a word, she typed another text to Kyle.

"Here's another thought," Zack added. "What if he doesn't go straight home? What if he drives out to the boondocks with the intent of killing another woman?"

"Then we follow him," Jenny replied. "And, hopefully, he will recognize he's being followed and he won't go through with it."

The make and model of Mark's car, along with the license plate number, came through in a text. Jenny showed Zack the screen before she continued, "If he does go home, I'm thinking we can stake him out…sit in front of his house and make sure he doesn't go anywhere. At least until sun up, that is, when we can be pretty sure he's not going to strike again any time soon."

"I'm glad we napped," Zack replied.

"You and me both."

Zack looked at his own phone and started poking around. He appeared to be shopping. "What are you doing?" Jenny asked.

"Seeing if we can find some kind of tracking device. I would like it better if we were able to keep tabs on his movements without having to actually follow him. Maybe tomorrow we can stick one of those bad boys on his car and then monitor him from somewhere else."

"We can do that?"

"That's what I'm trying to find out."

Jenny left him to his shopping, allowing her mind to wander. She couldn't wait to talk to Kyle to find out more information about Mark and Gary. She wondered what kind of background Mark had which would have led him to do such horrible things, and Gary was another story altogether. She had no idea who he was or how he fit into all of this, unless he was simply a friend of Mark's. She was inclined to dismiss him as a fraud, but Detective Brennan suggested he knew things about the crime scene that only the killer would know. But Mark had been the killer, at least according to Rachel. Was it possible that Mark had confided in Gary? But then why would Gary have been confessing? Why wouldn't Gary have implicated Mark instead of claiming that he was the one who had done it?

This whole thing stunk.

"It looks like they do sell tracking devices," Zack said. "They're supposed to be for your own car, but whatever."

"Does it have to go inside the car? Or can we stick it to the bumper or something?"

"We can ask. I think we need to go into a store and get one—I obviously don't want to wait for shipping. We'll just make sure we get one that can go on the outside of the car."

"Is that legal?" Jenny asked.

"Does it matter?"

Jenny smiled. No, it didn't matter. She contemplated how many times she'd stretched the boundaries of the law in order to prevent murder. Of course, her actions were always justified, but she recognized that one of these days she was going to find herself sitting in a jail cell.

At least she could afford bail.

Zack left the bar for a short time to walk around and look for Mark's car. It was parked behind the building in a small, gravel lot, presumably for employees only. The only way out of the lot was a narrow alley that came out on a side street, so they would definitely be able to see him leave if they set up in an appropriate spot.

The night dragged on slowly as Jenny half-expected the police to arrive in droves at any moment, carting Mark away in handcuffs. It never happened. As closing time drew near, she and Zack went out to their car—which hadn't been vandalized in any way—and drove away. After circling the block, they pulled onto the street near the employee lot.

"And now, we wait," Zack said.

Normally, Jenny hated those words, but she knew her wait was relatively short this time. The bar closed at two, and the staff probably had to stick around to help clean up after that, but she imagined Mark would be leaving the bar before three. With a sigh, she nestled into the driver's seat, leaned her head back and began watching the lot.

"This would be a whole lot easier if that Gary guy hadn't confessed," Jenny said. "Then the police could be doing this and we could be back at the hotel sleeping."

"Do you think the police would take your word for it and send somebody out here?"

"Well, considering twelve hours ago they had no suspects at all, I'd think they'd spare a lone patrolman to come out here and at least take a look. Besides, the chief takes me very seriously for some reason." She wiped her tired eyes. "This confession is just throwing a poorly-timed wrench in the works. Detective Brennan clearly thinks the confession is legit, so I imagine the entire force is either tasked with investigating Gary Kimbrough or getting some long overdue sleep, taking comfort in the fact that this nightmare is most likely behind them."

"Hopefully, it will be soon."

Jenny thought about going home and squeezing her son. "Hopefully, it will be."

"You know what this means, though, don't you? Scott Sweigert is just an unfortunate guy who lost both a coworker and a potential girlfriend to the same killer."

"And Jason is just a man with a very sick wife who flirts with young women to stay sane. And Luke is just a guy with big feet who happened to live upstairs from the first victim, and was potentially the object of another victim's crush. Every one of those guys suffered a loss, and the cloud of suspicion around them just added insult to injury."

"They'll understand, I think, eventually. If they cared about the women at all, they should be glad that the police are investigating every possibility."

"Imagine being in their shoes, though. Not only would it be scary—a little shoddy police work could land you in jail—but you know you're innocent, and the police are wasting valuable time giving you the third degree. It has to be frustrating to proclaim your innocence over and over and over again, only to have the police not believe you."

"The problem is that the guilty also proclaim their innocence over and over and over. You can't take the suspects at face value; otherwise everyone would walk out free."

"I guess not," Jenny replied. "I just can't imagine losing someone I loved and then getting accused of murdering them. That's a horrible double whammy."

"Maybe that's why Scott is still nursing a hangover right now."

"Oh, that poor guy. He was about as drunk as I've ever seen anybody."

"I can't say I blame him. I'd probably drink myself silly if I were in his shoes, too." After a short moment of silence, Zack added, "This is boring."

"Get used to it, my friend. This is how we're spending the whole night...hopefully. Either that, or he's going to try to strike again and we're going to have a night that is a little too exciting for my liking." Jenny thought all about the ways the evening could unfold. "Let's hope we spend the night staring at a parked car."

At two-forty-five, employees started coming out the back door of the bar, causing Jenny to sit up straighter in her seat. Silhouettes were all that could be seen, lit up by the street light above, but she was able to make out the bouncer due to his height. "Looks like the action is starting," she noted.

The employees waved emphatic goodbyes to each other, and their laughter was loud enough for Zack and Jenny to hear through the closed windows. "His coworkers seem to like him," Zack observed.

"Yeah, he's a real upstanding guy," she replied sarcastically.

Ignitions started throughout the lot, and Jenny followed suit, hoping nobody would notice them. Fortunately, nobody seemed to. Cars exited the lot in a single file line. Although it took some uncharacteristically aggressive driving on her part, Jenny managed to get behind Mark's car on the way out.

"Well done," Zack said, obviously impressed.

"I can drive obnoxiously when I need to."

She followed Mark's car, which turned right out of the lot—the direction he would have needed to go in order to get home. After a short drive, Mark parallel parked on a street in front of some townhouses, which Jenny recognized to be the road he lived on. He nonchalantly got out of the car, spinning his keys around his finger, and went into his house. The door closed. Lights turned on.

Everything seemed normal.

She found a parking space just down the road from his. Her heart was racing, but she said, "That was uneventful, thank goodness. I'm not really in the mood to take down a serial killer tonight."

Zack shrugged. "Eh. Maybe tomorrow."

"So, do you want to sleep the first shift, or should I?"

"You go ahead," he replied. "I'm still good and awake."

"Sounds good to me. I could actually deal with a few z's." She poked her husband on the shoulder. "I'm serious...if you fall asleep on the job, I will kill you."

"If I get sleepy, I will wake you, I promise. I know what's at stake, here. I won't fail."

She thought about when the baby was first born and Zack's inability to do overnight duty without falling asleep on the job. She doubted she would be able to get any decent rest; she would inevitably wake every ten minutes to make sure Zack's eyes were still open. This was going to be a long night.

After drifting off for a short time, Jenny's phone rang, causing her to jump to attention. Although her eyesight was blurry, she could see Kyle was calling. "Hello?"

"Jenny, it's Kyle. Sorry to wake you."

"No, it's okay. I wasn't really sleeping that soundly anyway. What's going on?"

"I found out some information about Mark Neighbors and Gary Kimbrough. Considering the guy strikes at night, I figured you needed this information as soon as possible, just in case he was thinking about doing it again tonight."

"No, that's perfect. What have you got?"

"Do you have the time? I don't want to interrupt anything."

Sitting up straighter, Jenny said, "Tonight, my friend, I've got nothing but time."

Chapter 17

"Gary Kimbrough, twenty-one, lives in Bennett with his aunt, Anita Rosencrance. I looked into his background a little bit; he's had a bit of a troubled past. His father never lived in the same state as he did, and his mother surrendered him to foster care when he was three years old. His mother has had several arrests for drugs since then, and is currently serving five years for selling marijuana to an undercover cop."

"Oh, dear," Jenny said.

"Gary bounced around in the foster care system for a while, until he came to live with his aunt when he was sixteen. This aunt is his father's sister, mind you. They had never met before he moved in with her."

"It was admirable of her to take him in."

"Agreed. He's had a few run-ins with the law himself—possession of marijuana, a couple of theft charges. Nothing big like murder, though."

"Were any of those charges recent? Or was that all back when he was younger?"

"Nothing in the past year and a half. He either hasn't gotten caught or he's cleaning up his act."

"Does he work?" Jenny asked.

"He works at a big-chain department store, probably earning minimum wage or close to it."

"What about religion?"

"I wasn't able to find anything about religion on this guy...the other guy? Tons."

"Before we move on to the other guy," Jenny began, "can you give me a physical description of Gary?"

"He's Caucasian, five-foot-ten, two-hundred-ten pounds, according to his driver's license. Brown hair, brown eyes. I can send you his license picture if you want."

"That would be great," Jenny replied, envisioning this stocky man of average height. "Maybe one of the girls will recognize him. Okay, how about Mark Neighbors?"

"Mark was born and raised in rural Pennsylvania. He's twenty-eight, also Caucasian, living at Hazel Drive in Bennett."

"I'm well aware of that," Jenny remarked. "I'm parked in front of his house right now."

"I'm going to pretend I don't know that for the next few minutes," Kyle said dryly. "Then, the father in me is going to ask you to explain yourself."

Jenny only smiled.

"Mark's parents were members of a religious sect called Messengers of God. They're an interesting group—very strict, denouncing such things as promiscuous dress, pre-marital sex...even make-up."

"And alcohol?"

"And alcohol. The group's leader is Reverend Artis Blakely, who is now in his seventies, but is still actively in charge. You'll notice I called this group a *sect* rather than a *cult*. They are extreme in their thinking, but they have no history of violence. The members are there voluntarily, and there is no brainwashing or recruiting of minors or anything like that. In fact, they do good things—a lot of work for the poor."

Jenny hung her head, wondering how this reverend would feel if he knew one of his members took it upon himself to rid the world of women who, in his mind, drank too much.

"As far as Mark himself is concerned, he has no criminal history. He graduated high school and went to work in a feed store, which was probably a popular place in the area where he is from. He just left that job six months ago, moving straight to where he is now. There is something interesting about him, though..."

"What is that?"

"He got married rather young, and his wife just filed for divorce shortly before he moved here."

Chills ran up Jenny's spine. "Divorce? Wouldn't that be frowned upon amongst the Messengers of God?"

"Oh, absolutely. I'm thinking that's why he left. And there's another thing...his soon-to-be-ex-wife has two DUI's now. Somehow I don't think she was all that keen on the rules of the Messengers of God."

As the pieces clicked into place in Jenny's brain, she was now absolutely convinced that she had the right person. "You, Kyle Buchanan, are my hero. Do you know that?"

"Did I say something right?"

"You sure did. I didn't tell you what was going on around here, but there's a guy running around slitting young women's throats in their sleep."

"Yeah, I'd heard about that. I figured you were part of the investigation."

"Well, the last girl lived long enough to hear the killer whisper in her ear...something about alcohol being from the devil, and then he said, 'May God accept you and keep you, despite your sins.' She recognized the voice to be Mark's, and it seems the one thing all three victims had in common was that they drank quite a bit."

"Oh, dear."

"Exactly. It kind of fits now, doesn't it? His wife was apparently a drinker and then filed for divorce. It sounds like she embodied the opposite of everything that the Messengers of God believe in. My guess would be that she wasn't like that when he married her; otherwise, he wouldn't have married her. I'm thinking she probably became that way over time. That would surely have been upsetting to him. In fact, it might have pushed him over the edge enough for him to go on a crusade against other women who remind him of her."

"I saw that he works for a bar now," Kyle added. "He probably sees plenty of women who drink too much."

"As the bouncer, no less...where he gets to look at driver's licenses that have people's addresses on them. He knows right where these women live."

"My God," Kyle whispered. With renewed vigor, he added, "And you are sitting in front of his house right now?"

"My husband and I are, yes. We are making sure he doesn't go anywhere."

"Isn't that a job for the police?"

"Well, there's a small little glitch that we've run into...someone else confessed earlier today—someone who knows details about the crime scene that only the killer would know."

"Is it safe for me to assume that was Gary?"

"It was. I have no idea how he fits into all of this, or how he might know details, but I am convinced now more than ever that Mark is the killer. But the police aren't looking for the killer anymore—they think they already have him."

"Which explains why you are sitting in front of Mark's house, keeping tabs on him."

"Yup. You got it."

"Are you sure you're safe?"

"Honestly, it doesn't look like he's going anywhere tonight. It's, what, four in the morning? I imagine he's sleeping right now. Tomorrow we're going to put a tracking device on his car so we can monitor him from a much safer distance. And speaking of cars...I have a confession to make, but I don't want you to be mad."

"What is it?"

Jenny sighed, reluctant to admit the truth. "Somebody has been messing with my car up here...slitting the tires, leaving notes on it—they even left a note on our hotel door."

"Oh, God, Jenny."

"I told you I don't want you to be mad."

He let out an impatient sigh. "What did the notes say?"

"Nothing, that's the weird part. They were just smiley faces."

Kyle grunted, remaining silent for several moments after that. "Believe it or not, that's pretty typical behavior for stalkers."

Jenny swallowed nervously. "It is?"

"Yeah. They like to leave calling cards, at least at first. Just little messages that say, *I've been here.* It's a psychological thing—they want to get inside their victim's head. In fact, I've known of stalkers who have broken into people's houses only to rearrange the furniture. They don't take anything; they don't hurt anyone; they just want the person to come home and be freaked out."

"Well, it works."

"I know it does. The problem is that the contacts usually become progressively more violent. It starts out small, but it can escalate to a frightening level very quickly."

"Great," Jenny said.

"I know. That's why I'm troubled by this. And I know what I'm talking about; I've been hired by more than one stalking victim over the years. Sometimes the victim knows exactly who the stalker is; other times they have no idea. It's bizarre what can trigger somebody to become obsessed. Some people have become stalking victims after only a brief, random encounter, like a lunch customer comes in and then devotes his life to following the waitress."

"Even though I don't know who it is specifically, I am under the impression that it's somebody related to the case. My Tennessee tags probably stood out like a sore thumb at the crime scenes, and my picture—and my *purpose*—were mentioned in the news for everyone to see."

"I wish you had told me this earlier. I could have come up there and kept an eye on both you and your car."

"That's so sweet of you, but I've been trying to figure it out on my own. We saw a surveillance tape of the guy, but it was night time, and we could only see his outline. He appeared to be average height and somewhat stocky—like the way you described Gary Kimbrough. But what I can't figure out is why Gary would have confessed, but he didn't turn Mark in along with him. Rachel has no doubt that Mark is the one who actually killed her, even if Gary was in on the planning." She shook her head. "If Gary's conscience was bothering him, I'd think he'd want to implicate everybody involved—especially the person who did the actual killing."

"It may be that Gary's conscience was bothering him, but there is also such a thing as a false confession," Kyle began.

"I know...I remember what you said before. That was my first impression—that he was just some guy looking for attention. But the detective said he knows things about the crime scene that they hadn't released to the public. How would he know that stuff if he isn't involved?"

Kyle remained quiet for a moment, ultimately saying, "Let me look into that. In the meantime, be careful. Don't develop a false sense of security just because this guy is only leaving smiley face notes. Like I said before, things can get ugly very quickly—it might be that he just wants to toy with you for a little while before going in for the kill—literally. So I'll say it again, please be careful."

"Well, Gary is in police custody right now. He confessed to the killings, so he can't do anything to me tonight."

"Are you positive that Gary is the person who's been stalking you?"

"Well, not *positive*."

"And you're right outside Mark's house, is that correct?"

"Yes, but he went in the house and hasn't come back out. We've been keeping an eye on him."

"Are you sure he didn't sneak out the back door and is approaching your car as we speak?"

Jenny froze. "Uh...no."

"You're full of nothing but good intentions, Jenny, but you are inexperienced as a private investigator. You are dealing with a psycho who has proven he's capable of murder. This isn't a game. As much as I hate to say it, part of me wants you to go back to your hotel—actually, a different hotel, where nobody knows where you'll be—and call it a night."

"I appreciate your concern, but I don't think Mark knows we're out here. Truly."

"He may not," Kyle replied, "but remember...it appears he's not working alone."

Chapter 18

Kyle's ominous warning ran through Jenny's mind until the sun began to peek over the horizon. As the black sky gave way to gray, Jenny turned the key and headed to the police station, optimistic that Mark hadn't done anything horrible overnight.

Unless he had snuck out the back door and killed a neighbor.

Jenny tried not to think about that as she pulled into the parking lot of the station. Instead, she focused her attention on Zack, who had finally drifted off in the passenger seat. He'd been up most of the night and deserved to sleep, but she didn't want to leave him alone in the car. However, they were at the police station, and she doubted anyone would have assaulted him there. It was cool outside, so leaving him in a locked car with the windows up wasn't a problem. All things considered, she decided to let him sleep.

She tried to ignore how tired she was as she got out of the car and headed toward the building. While she had gone one night without much sleep, the officers had gone many. She had less to complain about than anyone else in the building, so she sucked in some air, held her head high and pressed on.

Approaching the front desk, she stated her name and her business, asking to be put in touch with one of the investigators on the case. Detective Brennan was apparently home sleeping, so another detective came out to greet Jenny. She hoped this wouldn't be a problem; not everyone would have been as accepting of her abilities as Detective Brennan had been.

The man introduced himself as Detective Duffin, reaching out his hand with a big smile. Jenny deduced he was friendly enough, even if he did turn out to be a skeptic.

"Chief DePalo will be glad you're here," the detective began, sweeping his arm to indicate which direction Jenny should walk. "He wants you to talk to our suspect—see if you can shed any light on this."

"Sorry it took me so long to get here," she replied. "I had some stuff to take care of."

"That's okay," he said. "I didn't want to mention it, but you look like you've had a long night."

Jenny smiled, realizing what a brave comment that was for him to make. "I did, but nothing compared to what you guys have been dealing with."

With a laugh, he said, "Yeah, thank goodness for coffee. I think I have more coffee in my system than blood right now."

They wandered through some hallways, landing in a small room that Jenny presumed was for interrogation purposes. "Why don't you have a seat," he began. "I'll let the chief know you're here, and then we'll see about getting Kimbrough out here for you."

She nodded and smiled politely. "Sounds good." After Detective Duffin left her alone, she looked around the room, unable to stifle the shudder that worked its way up her back. Some terrible things had been described within the confines of these four walls. Peoples' freedom had come to an end here. She was glad that she was there on the correct side of the law, although she knew, one day, she might not be.

She needed to be careful with her *law bending*.

The chief rounded the corner in his suit and tie, which remained remarkably crisp compared to the exhaustion evident on his face. However, mixed with the fatigue was an air of triumph, which Jenny feared was misguided. She felt bad that she was about to call the arrest they'd made into question, especially considering he seemed so proud of it.

"Jenny," he said, smiling, "thanks for coming out this morning."

She stood, extending her hand. "No problem, Chief DePalo. I'm happy to help."

He took a clumsy seat across from her, his weight plopping down awkwardly, most likely because he didn't have the energy to sit gracefully. He leaned back in the chair and sighed loudly, announcing, "I assume you've heard about the confession."

"Yes, sir, I have."

"I want you to meet him...let me know what you think."

"I'd be happy to, but..." she began, biting her lip with a moment of hesitation, "I do have some things I need to tell you first."

"Okay, shoot."

She didn't want to *shoot*, but she knew she had to. "As you know, Rachel Moore heard the killer's voice before she died. She knew it was familiar, but she couldn't place it for a long time. It took her a while, but she finally realized it was the bouncer at Shenanigans."

The look of triumph on the chief's face disappeared, replaced by a serious glare. "The man who confessed is not a bouncer at Shenanigans."

"I know," Jenny said sheepishly. "That's my concern. I think the person who committed the crime—at least Rachel's—is named Mark Neighbors. I got a private investigator friend of mine to look into his history, and he was born into a very religious family with old fashioned values. He married young, probably intending to uphold those values, but then his wife got a few drunk-driving arrests and filed for divorce. He must have been not only heartbroken by that, but humiliated as well. I'm thinking that's the reason he's gone on this rampage—to kill women that remind him of his soon-to-be-ex-wife."

Chief DePalo rubbed the back of his neck as he exhaled loudly; his expression looked pained. "While that does sound plausible, you have to understand...the confession we have appears to be legit. There's no other explanation for it. He knows things that only the killer would know."

"I realize that," Jenny said without animosity in her voice, "and that's what I don't understand. It has occurred to me that maybe they were working together. Or maybe they were just friends, and Mark may have told Gary some details about the crime scene when he confided in him. But, either way, I'm convinced Mark Neighbors did the actual killing."

The chief looked like he was deep in thought; this was clearly a wrench he didn't want thrown in the works. She imagined a nice, tidy confession was the ending they'd all been hoping for. Sitting frozen, she waited for his reaction, which she hoped wasn't hostile.

He let out another deep breath, declaring, "I owe you a story."

Jenny remained silent, waiting for him to continue.

"I do believe in psychics. I do believe that the deceased have the ability to communicate." His eyes rose to meet hers, the intensity on his face intimidating. "I saw it first-hand, back when I was a kid. My parents got divorced when I was young, and my mom and I moved into a small house. It was a two-bedroom little thing. Two story. When you walked in the front door, the kitchen and dining room were to your left, the living room to your right, and a set of stairs in front of you. At the top of the stairs, there was a bedroom on either side and a bathroom in the middle." He used his hands to illustrate his description before crossing his arms over his chest. "My bedroom was the one on the right.

"I used to see a woman there," he continued. "Well, I didn't *see* her, but I felt her presence. I saw her shadows. I sensed her movements. I was afraid of her at first, but, after a while, I learned she wasn't going to hurt me. I just kind of accepted that her spirit lived in there, but I didn't tell my mom about it—at least, not for the first few years.

"When I was nine or ten, I mentioned it to my mother—that I sensed a presence in my room. I told her I had been aware of it since we'd moved in there. She was shocked to hear me say it, not because she didn't believe me, but because she'd experienced it, too. And that's when she told me."

Jenny's eyes remained locked on his.

He sighed deeply and added, "The previous owners had been a young couple with a baby boy. The father worked; the mother stayed home. The baby was probably about six months old when the husband came home and found his wife dead at the bottom of the stairs. The baby was screaming in his crib, his diaper soaking wet, and there was no sign of any foul play. The doors were locked. Nothing had been taken. Nothing was out of order. It's believed she fell down the steps after putting the baby down for his nap." He looked down toward the table. "The steps were made of wood, and she had socks on. It appears her feet slipped out from underneath her, and she hit the back of her head on one of the stairs." Continuing to look solemn, he added, "Her neck was broken."

Jenny put her hand over her mouth. Considering the age of her own baby, this story was hitting a little too close to home.

"The husband sold the house shortly after. He couldn't stand to walk past the spot where his wife had died, day in and day out. My mom bought if from him. She said she got a good deal on it. Apparently, nobody wanted to buy the house where the young mother had died.

"The room I moved into was the baby's room," he went on. "That was the only place either one of us had ever seen her spirit. My mother had assumed she was sticking around to make sure her baby was okay. Maybe she even thought I was her baby; I don't know. All I do know is that I felt her presence, long before I ever knew that she had died in that house." He sat up straighter and drew a breath. "Spirits are real, Jenny. I know that. And there's not a doubt in my mind that they can contact us. I'm not sure how you have the ability to hear it so clearly, but I don't doubt that it's true."

"It runs in my family," Jenny said softly.

"And I have nothing but respect for that ability." He leaned forward to speak with her more intimately. "But what I have here is a confession. A solid one. I realize you have insight that suggests someone else did this, but I have no tangible evidence at this point that would lead me in a different direction than the one I'm already headed."

"Rachel bled on her attacker. Her DNA would be on his gloves."

"I figured that, but Kimbrough said he disposed of the gloves—and his clothes, and the size fourteen shoes he wore to throw us off his trail. He put them in a bag, weighed them down and dropped them into the Appomac River. We've got dive teams looking for the bag now." Appearing apologetic, he added, "Honestly, Jenny, I do believe in your ability, but, at this time, I have no reason to think we've got it wrong."

Jenny nodded with understanding, fully aware that this man had nothing but good intentions. "I'd like to meet him," she replied quietly. "Kimbrough, I mean. I want to see if the girls recognize him."

Chief DePalo leaned back in his chair and smiled. "Excellent. Hopefully you can let me know what his affiliation was with these women. At this point, it seems like the victims were chosen randomly, but I wonder if there was something more to it than that."

Jenny had a few questions of her own that she wanted answered. "Sounds good," she replied. "Where do you need me to go?"

"The meeting can happen in here, if you'd like. We'll have him cuffed and shackled, and I can be in here with you to keep you safe. We'll have officers watching through a one-way mirror, too, so if he gets...excited...we can subdue him quickly."

"Actually, I'd prefer to be alone with him, if you don't mind." She tapped her temple. "Having fewer people in the room makes the connection easier." That wasn't exactly the truth, but the chief didn't need to know what her real reasons were.

He looked at her for a moment before saying, "Are you sure about that? He's a dangerous man."

In Jenny's mind, the only thing that made him dangerous was his interference with the investigation. That, and possibly his friendship with Mark Neighbors. "Absolutely," she replied. "Although, I will take you up on the offer to have officers watching through the mirror..."

Gary Kimbrough's steps were small due to the shackles on his ankles. His hands were cuffed to a chain around the waist of his orange jumpsuit. His hair was disheveled and his eyes half-closed, indicating he'd been woken up for the meeting. Considering the sun had just barely risen, that certainly could have been the case.

The guard instructed him to sit, and he did so without a word. "We will be standing right outside the room watching, so no funny business," the guard said, giving Gary a slight nudge on the shoulder. Turning to Jenny, he added, "If he gives you any trouble, or does anything to make you feel uncomfortable, just raise your hand. We'll be in here faster than you can bat an eye."

Jenny smiled pleasantly at the guard, thanking him, and watched him walk out the door. She fixed her gaze on Gary Kimbrough, the self-proclaimed killer, and waited for some kind of message from the victims—a vision, a memory—something. His face sparked no recognition, no fear, no anger, confirming Jenny's suspicion that this was not the man.

Her fatigue allowed her to be cool and emotionless when she spoke. "So, you're the killer."

He cocked his head to the side, wearing a tough expression. "That's right. And who are you?"

Jenny didn't let her eyes leave his. "I am a woman who knows the truth."

Chapter 19

Gary didn't flinch at Jenny's words; he simply continued to stare at her.

"I know you didn't do this, Gary. And you know you didn't do this. But here's the one thing that I can't figure out," she went on. "Why would somebody confess to a crime they didn't commit? Is it for the attention? Low self-esteem? What is it? Care to enlighten me?"

Looking cocky, he replied, "I wouldn't know."

She was too tired for this. "You wouldn't know." She said it more like a sentence than a question.

"Nope. Sure wouldn't."

She rubbed her eyes in an attempt to regroup. After her hands worked their way down her face and clasped under her chin, she leaned forward on the table that separated her from Gary. "How long to you plan to keep this up?"

He simply shrugged and looked at her as if he were challenging her.

"Okay, then, tell me...how long have you known Mark?"

He scoffed. "Mark who?"

"You don't know anyone named Mark?"

"I know a couple of guys named Mark."

"Well, I would think you'd know which one I was talking about here. After all, he played an integral role in the murders."

"There was no *Mark* involved with the murders."

"That's not what Rachel Moore told me."

Gary didn't reply, leading Jenny to believe she'd left him without anything to say.

"See, that's what you may not understand. Those three young women? They can talk to me. I can hear them. And Rachel knows who did this to her, and she knows it wasn't you."

He continued to remain silent.

"I'm not sure exactly what your goal is, but let me make something clear to you." She tapped her finger on the table. "While you're in here getting your ego stroked by all this attention, the real killer is out there, probably planning to strike again. And you know what? The police aren't even looking for him anymore, because they have you. So make no mistake about it—while you didn't kill these women that you're claiming to have killed, you are definitely responsible for the death of the next one. Can you really live with that?"

"You don't know what you're talking about."

"Okay, then, what was your motive?"

He shrugged one shoulder. "I can't really say. Something just came over me."

"Why these women?"

"They were convenient."

"How are you going to explain it when the cops can't find that *bag* with the clothes and shoes in it?" She used finger quotes.

"Incompetence."

"What about the smiley-face notes?"

For a brief moment, his face showed a hint of confusion. He quickly recovered, stating, "I don't want to talk about that."

Confusion. He didn't know anything about the notes. Jenny felt her blood run cold, realizing this man in front of her wasn't the stocky man who had been harassing her.

If it wasn't him, then who was it?

"Well, I don't have the time to waste on you," Jenny replied calmly, beginning to stand up. "I've got to go make sure the killer doesn't strike again."

"I won't," Gary said coolly.

Jenny rolled her eyes. "You never did."

Before she even reached the door, the guards came in. "Are you okay, ma'am?" one of them asked, the worry apparent in his voice.

"Yes," Jenny replied with a smile, "This interview is just over. And I won't be needing him anymore; I've got everything I need from this young man."

The guard who spoke then placed his hand on Gary's elbow. "Come on, tough guy," he said, "back to your cell."

Gary stood up, taking baby steps out of the room. He didn't even glance in Jenny's direction as he left.

She found herself alone for only a short moment before Chief DePalo came back in. Closing the door behind him, he looked at Jenny eagerly. "Did you get any insight?"

"Yes and no," she replied with her head down. She braced herself before she continued, "The girls said nothing to me, which actually told me a lot. I hate to tell you this, but I truly believe he's the wrong man. I am convinced, now more than ever, that your guy is Mark Neighbors. He had the means and the motive...and feet big enough to need a size fourteen shoe."

The chief let out a sigh, looking genuinely torn. "I'm sorry you feel that way. I really wish we were on the same page."

"I'm sorry, too." Jenny looked up at the tall police chief in front of her. "I'm sorry that Gary Kimbrough has led you astray."

Climbing back into her car, Jenny shook Zack's shoulder before she turned the key. "Wake up, sleepyhead. We've got things to do."

With a loud groan and a stretch, he asked, "What time is it?"

"About seven-thirty."

"Huh," he replied, obviously confused. "I must have fallen asleep."

"You did, and I'm glad you did. You needed it. But now we have some errands to run. I looked last night, and, unfortunately, the stores that sell the tracking devices don't open until ten, but we have another mission to accomplish before that."

He tilted his head back and forth, invoking a loud pop in his neck. "Holy crap, I feel like a pretzel. I'm not young enough to sleep in a car anymore."

"Well, once we get these few things taken care of, we can go back to the hotel and sleep in a bed...and I, for one, can't wait."

He let out a yell with another full body stretch. "Where are we headed?"

"Buford Park," she replied, glancing at the clock. "I just hope we get there in time to catch the delivery of a biscuit with sausage and eggs."

As they walked down the path at Buford Park, Jenny was so tired that she felt like she was having an out-of-body experience. She went through the motions of taking steps, but her brain hadn't gotten out of the car yet. Joggers whizzed by in both directions, full of energy, apparently well-rested after a full night's sleep. She found herself painfully jealous of their vigor.

Before too long, the homeless man came into sight. He was sitting along the path again, in almost the exact same spot as last time. He was alone, which made Jenny slightly nervous; she hoped Jeremy hadn't already come and gone.

"Hello, Sir Walter James Southerland the Third," she said cheerfully once they were within earshot.

He looked up at her. "Hello, Pam."

Pam?

Keeping the smile on her face, she replied, "My name isn't Pam."

"You look like a Pam."

"I do, huh?" Jenny didn't realize that *Pam* had a look.

Zack seemed amused by this conversation. "What do I look like?"

Sir Walter James Southerland the Third gave him the once-over. "You look like a man who could use more sleep."

Zack and Jenny both laughed out loud. "You hit the nail on the head, there, friend," Zack replied. "Last night was a rough one."

"So, what brings you all back out here this morning?"

"We just wanted to talk," Jenny said.

A jogger ran by, raising his hand in a hello to Sir Walter James Southerland the Third, who returned the gesture. "Well, have a seat," he replied, waving his arm out to the side. "I haven't cleaned today, though."

Stifling a smile, Jenny said, "That's okay. No need to clean for us." Finding a decent-sized rock, she sat her bottom down and curled her legs into her chest. The rock was cold, damp and hard, but she was not about to complain. She could tolerate a few minutes of this, considering the man next to her lived under these conditions all the time. "I actually have a question for you, my friend," she continued.

"Is it a math question?"

"A math question?" Jenny repeated with surprise. "No, it's not a math question."

"That's probably best," Sir Walter James Southerland the Third confessed. "My skills are a bit rusty these days."

Jenny liked this guy. "My question is a bit more personal than a math question. Here's what I want to know: if you had the opportunity to live somewhere...in a house, I mean...would you like that?"

"In a house?"

"Yeah," Jenny said, "instead of outside. You wouldn't have to deal with the heat or the cold or the rain. You could shower, and you'd have a bathroom."

"Right now, the world is my bathroom," he replied with a smile, gesturing to the trees behind him.

"You know, there is beauty in that," Zack noted.

Jenny looked at her husband strangely, shaking her head. Focusing her attention back on the homeless man, she asked, "Would that interest you, Sir? Having a bathroom, and a bed, and a warm place to stay?"

"I had a bed once." He nodded emphatically.

"You did?"

"Yup. About a week ago."

Jenny smiled. "Did you like having a bed?"

"I seem to recall that I did."

"Would you like to have a bed again?"

With a grin, he said, "Might be nice."

"I can arrange that for you, as it turns out. I'd just need you to come with either me or Jeremy to the place where you could live. They'll ask you some questions, but I think they'd let you stay."

He thought for a moment, sadly adding, "I wouldn't see the fawn get born."

"No, you wouldn't," Jenny agreed, "but maybe Jeremy can get a picture for you."

"The doe doesn't trust Jeremy. She trusts me. She won't let him close enough to her baby to get a picture."

In an instant, Jenny's perspective changed. Yes, Sir Walter James Southerland the Third had no official home, but that didn't mean his life was without highpoints. He had routines and relationships that he would inevitably miss—the man even considered the bugs to be his friends. While, to her, it seemed like the move indoors would be entirely positive, she hadn't taken into account his attachment to the things he'd be leaving behind. Perhaps, to him, the comfortable bed wouldn't be worth it.

"Maybe you can come visit," she said cheerfully. "Maybe Jeremy can bring you out here sometimes, and you can visit the doe yourself."

He frowned as he nodded. "A visit sounds nice."

Just as Jenny felt a bit of optimism at his words, her cell phone chirped. She lifted her phone out of her purse, talking a quick look at the screen. The text was from Kyle.

I've got Artis Blakely's contact information. If you can let him know your suspicions, maybe he can talk to Mark. Hopefully he is as non-violent as he seems, and he'll be able to get Mark to turn himself in. Or, at the very least, not kill again. A phone number followed.

In her tired state, it took Jenny an extra moment to remember who Artis Blakely was—but then it hit her. He was the leader of the religious sect that Mark had belonged to back in Pennsylvania. She was excited to get that information, and a little bit disappointed in herself that she hadn't thought to ask for it. If anybody could have gotten Mark to stop the killing, it would have been Artis Blakely.

Although, this new information meant she may have to postpone that nap she wanted so desperately. *Oh, well,* she thought. *Save lives first; sleep later.*

She dropped her phone back into her purse, returning her attention to Sir Walter James Southerland the Third and Zack, who had been chatting while she wasn't paying attention. Behind them, in the distance, she saw Jeremy heading in their direction. "Is that your breakfast, Sir Walter James Southerland the Third?"

He glanced down the trail, announcing, "Yup. That'd be it."

After Jeremy got a little closer, Jenny waved to him, and he raised the bag of food as a return hello. His smile was broad—perhaps seeing Jenny and Zack there gave him hope that they were actually going to fulfill their promise and provide his friend with a home.

"Good morning," he said cheerfully. "I was hoping to see you two here today."

"We're here," Jenny replied. "I'm not sure how awake we are, but we're here."

Handing a bag over to Sir Walter James Southerland the Third, he said, "One biscuit with sausage and eggs."

"Thank you, kindly."

"And one jug of water."

"Thank you again."

"And now for a little scripture. What would you like to hear today?"

After a moment of thought, the homeless man suggested, "How about a little something about friendship, in honor of my two new friends?"

"Okay," Jeremy said, "friendship it is." Bowing his head, he said, "Two are better than one because they have a good return for their labor. For if either of them falls, the one will lift up his companion. But woe to the one who falls when there is not another to lift him up."

Jenny felt her breath catch as she thought about Mick and John and their quest for sobriety.

Her sentiments were short lived, however; the homeless man's voice snapped her back into the present. "Nice one. What was that?"

"Ecclesiastes four, nine and ten," Jeremy told him.

"I like that one."

"Me, too." Jeremy opened up his breakfast wrapper and took a bite of his sandwich.

"We were just telling Sir Walter James Southerland the Third about the possibility of living indoors," Zack explained to Jeremy. "He seems like he might be on board with the idea."

Jeremy's expression was a mixture of awe and happiness. "This is unbelievable." Turning to his friend, he asked, "You up for that?"

Sir Walter James Southerland the Third frowned and gave one emphatic nod. "I don't see why not."

"I'd like to show you the place I found for him, if that's okay," Zack said to Jeremy.

"I'd love to see it."

Pulling out his phone, Zack scrolled and swiped as he said, "It's called White Oak Psychiatric, and it's about twenty minutes from here." After a few more taps, he held out his phone for Jeremy to see. "Here's a picture of the place; it looks like a nice facility."

Jeremy raised his eyebrows, appearing to battle tears. "A lot better than the accommodations he has now."

Zack smiled and clicked a few links, turning the phone back to Jeremy. "Here's a picture of the rooms; they're dorm style. They're pretty small, but he'd have a bed and a private bathroom. There's a nurse's station on every floor, and they have a cafeteria in the lobby. They are also fully staffed with doctors to monitor his progress and medications."

Jeremy ran his hand over his dreadlocks, which were neatly pulled back in a band. "I don't even know what to say."

Jenny couldn't help but smile at how touched he looked. "He does have some concerns, though," she added. "He's a little worried about not getting to see the fawn after it's born. Would you be willing to take him back here from time to time so he can say hello?"

"Of course I would. I'm not going to forget about him just because he's got a roof over his head." He softened his voice so that Sir Walter James Southerland the Third couldn't hear. "I think I'm the only one who visits him."

Jenny wanted to hug Jeremy, but she used restraint. She also wanted to hold a big, neon sign over his head that said, *If you are smart, you will marry this man,* complete with flashing arrows and light bulbs pointing in Jeremy's direction. For a moment, she wondered how many Jeremys she had walked past in her youth while she was arm-in-arm with a selfish football player, feeling like she'd hit the relationship jackpot because the guy next to her was popular and had muscles. Oh, to go back in time and kick herself in the head.

"But, how is he going to afford this?" Jeremy asked, snapping Jenny out of her train of thought.

"Don't worry about that," Jenny replied. "It's not an issue."

Jeremy reached out and touched her shoulder, patting it a few times in different places. When she looked at him curiously, he replied, "I just want to make sure you're real."

Laughing out loud, she said, "Yes, I'm real." She explained her unique situation of having received a sizeable inheritance, with the explicit instructions that she use the money to help people. "Your friend, here, is the perfect candidate, if you ask me. He seems like such a kind soul, but he doesn't have the means to take care of himself."

"You got it," Jeremy said. "That's him to a T."

"You guys are doing a lot of talking over there," Sir Walter James Southerland the Third said as he took a bite of his breakfast.

Jeremy smiled. "We're trying to arrange it so you can have a place to stay."

The homeless man held up his sandwich. "Carry on, then."

With a genuine laugh, Jeremy focused his attention back on Jenny. "Have you noticed how well-spoken he is? He doesn't always make the most sense, but his grammar is excellent, which leads me to believe he is a highly educated man." He shook his head. "I wonder who he used to be before he came to live out here."

If Jenny hadn't already resolved herself to helping him, she would have been heartbroken by the comment. "I have come into contact with the mentally ill in the past, and I learned that a lot of the disorders are adult-onset. It's so sad to think that a kid grows up, goes to college or learns a trade, maybe gets married...only to have it all fall apart. It's unimaginable to me, really. We have a baby at home, and he seems perfectly healthy—but there's a chance that thirty years from now he'll be out here living in the park?" She, too, shook her head. "I can't wrap my head around that."

"Well, hopefully, you won't ever have to," Jeremy said.

She crossed her fingers, looking intently at him. "Life is such a crap shoot. So far, I've managed to come out on the lucky end of just about everything...I don't know how."

"God is good," Jeremy replied with a smile.

"God *is* good," she agreed, "but there are still men like Sir Walter James Southerland the Third walking the earth."

"And there are people like you to help him," Jeremy pointed out. "You will never convince me that God didn't have you cross paths for a reason."

She wasn't about to argue with such a wonderful man, but the reason she was in Bennett, Missouri to begin with was to catch a serial killer. What could possibly have been the explanation for that? Did God make mistakes, just like everyone else?

Jenny stopped that train of thought. Now was neither the time nor the place for such negativity. Instead, she smiled politely and said, "The same can be said for you, my friend. In case no one has said it before, thank you for everything you've done for him."

"It's the Christian thing to do."

This time, Jenny couldn't resist the urge. "Come here," she said, reaching her arm up and around Jeremy's neck. "You are such a sweet soul."

They engaged in a friendly embrace for only a short time before they heard Sir Walter James Southerland the Third say, "It looks like there's a lot of love around here."

She couldn't help but laugh, looking affectionately at the man whose life was about to change dramatically. "Yeah, there is a lot of love out here."

The foursome spent the next twenty minutes talking logistics, ending with Sir Walter James Southerland the Third going back into the woods to retrieve his things. While Jenny wondered what his *things* could have possibly consisted of, she realized his possessions were probably dear to him, and they should absolutely go with him to his new home. Jeremy agreed to drive him to White Oak Psychiatric once he returned from the woods, and a quick phone call from Jenny arranged the first payment.

Sir Walter James Southerland the Third emerged from the trees with an old blanket used like a sack to contain clanking items inside it. "You ready?" Jeremy asked. "I think some wonderful opportunities await you."

He squinted as he looked back into the trees. "Yes, I do think I am."

Jenny blinked back her tears once they all reached the parking lot. She bid her goodbyes to the two men, sincerely wishing them both the best of luck in the future.

Her heart sang as she watched the soon-to-be-not-homeless man load his things into Jeremy's trunk. Once inside the car, Jeremy helped Sir Walter negotiate the seatbelt into place before hooking up his own. When Jeremy spun around in the driver's seat so he could reverse the car, he looked up at Jenny and Zack one last time, giving them a broad smile and a peace sign before focusing on the road.

Waving goodbye, Jenny watched the car back out of the space and drive off down the road. And just like that, they were gone. Sir Walter James Southerland the Third was about to begin a new chapter of his life.

Taking one more second to enjoy the moment, she sucked in a deep breath, releasing it slowly. She just needed a few more seconds of this feeling before she focused on the horrible matter ahead of her.

After giving herself a little time, she turned to her husband and asked, "Do you mind driving to the electronics store?"

"No, I don't mind. Do you trust me?"

She was positive this was a reference to his previous speeding ticket. "Drive slow."

She tossed him the keys from her purse as she pulled out her phone. Plopping into the passenger seat, she jotted down the contact information Kyle had sent in his text. After pressing a few buttons, she held the phone to her ear and heard the male voice answer, "Reverend Blakely."

Chapter 20

"Hello, Reverend Blakely, my name is Jenny Larrabee, and I am calling from Bennett, Missouri."

"Well, what can I do for you this fine morning, Ms. Larrabee?"

For the millionth time, she found herself wishing she had rehearsed something before she dialed the phone. She wondered if she'd ever learn. "I wanted to discuss one of your parishioners with you, if you don't mind."

"Well, that depends who you are and what you want to know."

Jenny hadn't started this off very well. "I am working with the police here on a murder investigation; my goal with this conversation is to save some lives."

"Well, then, I'm happy to help...although, I have to admit, I don't know how a member of my congregation would fit into a murder investigation in Missouri."

She closed her eyes tightly, realizing there was no tactful way to state the reason for her call. "It's about Mark Neighbors, who lives in this area now, and he's..."

"Mark Neighbors is *not* a Messenger of God."

Jenny sat speechlessly for a moment, wondering how to respond to that. The reverend's tone suggested that Jenny hadn't simply been mistaken, but rather there was hostility involved. "I'm sorry; I was under the impression that he was."

"He used to be, but he most definitely is not anymore."

"May I ask why he is no longer a member?"

His voice sounded professional and rehearsed. "Ms. Larrabee, we Messengers of God live by certain doctrines; there are acceptable behaviors, and there are unacceptable behaviors. Mr. Neighbors clearly showed no regard for our principles here at the church, and, for that reason, he has been dismissed as a member."

Dismissed. That certainly explained some things, although, to Jenny, one aspect remained unclear. "I realize your beliefs don't permit drinking or divorce, but I am fairly certain that Mark doesn't drink, and the divorce wasn't his idea."

"I suppose you are hearing the story from Mark's point of view."

"Actually, I'm getting it from more of a third party."

"Perhaps your *third party* is a little bit biased in their assessment."

Jenny silently waited for him to elaborate.

He let out a sigh before he continued, this time in a much more vulnerable tone. "Yes, his wife had issues with alcohol addiction. Yes, his wife filed for divorce. However, his wife was also the victim of domestic violence—at the hands of her husband—which is something we will absolutely not tolerate amongst our parishioners."

In an instant, Jenny's view of the *Messengers of God* changed completely. Perhaps they weren't as fanatical as she had once thought; maybe they frowned upon drinking and divorce, but they wouldn't necessarily banish someone for those offenses. Violence, on the other hand...

Reverend Blakely went on, "Don't get me wrong; we tried to help him. What we found, however, was that every time we suggested he have a counseling session with me, not only would he refuse, but his wife would show up the next day with fresh bruises. Of course, she always made some kind of excuse for them—you know, she fell down the stairs or whatnot—but we all knew the truth. Mark Neighbors was a wife beater, plain and simple, and we will not allow that here at the *Messengers of God.*"

"From what I understand, he doesn't have a criminal record," Jenny noted. "Does that mean he never faced any charges?"

"We could never get his wife to admit he was violent. Without her testimony, no charges would have ever stuck."

"I guess that does make sense," Jenny said with defeat.

"You say this is about a murder investigation," the reverend added, more like a statement than a question. "Are you under the impression that Mark killed somebody?"

"Several people, actually. Women who drink a lot. Women who, I assume, remind him of his soon-to-be-ex-wife."

"Sadly, that doesn't surprise me," he replied softly. "We actually feared he would end up killing his wife, which is why we wouldn't allow him on the premises. We let his wife stay here at the church so she could be safe, and we kept him as far away from her as possible. He ended up moving away, I'm guessing to Missouri. I'm just sorry that you all have to deal with him now."

"You and me both," she muttered. "I was actually calling you to see if you could have a talk with him. I was hoping he'd listen to you considering how strong his religious beliefs are and how respected you are among the *Messengers of God*."

"He's already proven that he won't listen to me—or to anybody else, for that matter. Any conversation we had with him only did more harm than good."

The disappointment was obvious in Jenny's voice when she replied, "I kind of figured."

"Pardon me for asking this," the reverend began, "but if you know he's killing these women, why don't you just arrest him?"

"The problem is that *I* know he's killing these women," Jenny said, "but I'm not a police officer. The police are under the impression that it's somebody else—a man who confessed yesterday. I'm trying to gather enough evidence so the cops will know they have the wrong man, but in the meantime, I'm also trying to make sure Mark doesn't kill anyone else. That's why I was hoping you could talk to him."

"Considering my talks always have the opposite effect, I'd rather not."

Jenny shook her head. "I know. I don't expect you to. I was just explaining my reasoning behind the call." She wiped her eyes with her free hand, realizing she had officially struck out. She did, however, hope to gain something from the call. "Can I ask you something else, while I have you on the phone?"

"Absolutely."

"How long have you known Mark?"

"His whole life," the reverend said.

"Then, what happened? I mean, how did he end up this way? Do you have any idea?"

Reverend Blakely let out a sigh. "I've asked myself that question many times. His parents are lovely people with three other children that have grown into wonderful, productive citizens. There's something about Mark, though, that has always been off. From the time he was little, something about him has been not quite right. His parents have known that, too, but they've never been able to put their finger on the problem."

"I've had a little experience with mental illness, so I understand," Jenny replied. "Although, I don't really think mental illness applies here. Mark doesn't seem to be withdrawn or incomprehensible or anything like that."

"Oh, I don't think he's mentally ill, either," Reverend Blakely said emphatically. "I think what we're dealing with here is a man who is just plain evil."

The words sent a chill down Jenny's spine. "I have to agree with you. And you think he was born this way?"

"I can't blame his upbringing; like I said, his parents are lovely people."

Jenny thought of her baby at home, hoping and praying that he had been born with all of the correct wiring. Trying to get her mind off of the thought, she remarked, "Okay, I have one more question, and then I can stop bothering you."

With a slight laugh, he said, "You're not bothering me."

"Well, I am just wondering how Mark's wife is doing now. Is she any better without him in her life?"

"She's flourishing," the reverend said proudly. "She just celebrated five months without a drink. It's amazing how well she can function without the constant fear of her husband losing his temper."

Jenny nodded; this was at least one piece of good news. "I'm happy to hear that," she replied honestly. "Now I just need to figure out a way to get this guy off the streets, and we'll be all set."

"Good luck with that," Reverend Blakely said. "The world will be a much safer place with him behind bars."

She concluded her call and told the story to Zack. "So, unfortunately, it looks like Reverend Blakely won't be able to get through to him after all."

"It was worth a shot," Zack noted. "He was the best chance we had."

"Yup," she replied as she looked helplessly out the window. "He sure was."

"Well, it looks like we have a little time before the electronics store opens. What do you want to do? Pull into a parking lot somewhere and grab a little nap?"

"Actually, I don't, believe it or not," she said, "for two reasons. First, if that guy is following us, we might be sitting ducks if we're both asleep in the car. Second, if I do fall asleep, I won't wake back up. I guarantee it. We don't have that long to wait; why don't we just go get a coffee instead?"

Zack turned the wheel, putting the car in the direction of the diner. "One coffee, coming right up."

Zack parked in the front of the diner this time, where the lot would be busy and their car wouldn't be victimized. They approached the diner's door, and Jenny found herself struck by a handwritten sign taped to the glass that said, "Closed from 8 a.m. to noon tomorrow for Lisa's funeral." In smaller print underneath, it read, "Please keep Lisa and her family in your prayers. If you have any information about her murder, please contact the police."

"Damn," Jenny whispered. Somehow, that sign made everything seem much more real.

Sensing her sadness, Zack placed his hand on her back, "That's why we're here. Hopefully, we can keep this from happening again."

"That won't be much consolation to the people who loved Lisa," she noted.

"You'd be surprised. If we can catch him, it just might make them feel better."

She nodded solemnly as they entered, quickly being led to a booth by the window. Once seated, she used her hands to keep her head up, her fatigue in full swing. "The last time I was here, Detective Brennan and I accused an innocent man of murdering women."

"Well, you didn't know."

Jenny thought about responding, but forming the words felt like too much effort.

The waitress came by, offering, "Can I start you off with a little coffee?"

"You can start us off with *a lot* of coffee," Jenny replied.

"Actually, can you set me up with an IV drip and just put it directly into my bloodstream?" Zack asked. "It would be more efficient."

The waitress laughed. "That bad, huh? Well, I'll get on that right away, then."

She disappeared, and Jenny began staring distantly out the window, focusing on nothing in particular.

"That guy," Zack began. "That pervert guy...what was his name again?"

Shifting her eyes to look at her husband, she proposed, "Jason?" She wanted to argue that he wasn't a pervert, but rather a man who had been dealt a crappy hand by life. Ultimately, though, the distinction didn't matter.

"Yeah, Jason. He was kind of a stocky guy, wasn't he?"

Jenny felt herself wake up a little bit. "You don't think he's the one who's been stalking us..."

"Somebody's doing it."

Somebody *was* doing it. "But why him?" Jenny asked. "What motive would he have?"

Throwing his hands up, Zack made a face to suggest he had no answer for that. "All I know is that somebody has been messing with you, and this guy was at the diner the same time our tires got slashed."

"But what on earth would he possibly have to gain?"

At that moment, two steaming cups of coffee, along with a carafe, appeared in front of them. Jenny placed her face over the cup, using her hands to whisk the scent toward her nose. "Oh my goodness, this smells amazing." Wasting no time, the couple prepared their coffees and started to drink. A few sips in, Jenny added, "I agree that Jason was stocky, but I can't imagine that he's the one who has been following us. I don't think he has anything to do with this at all. The problem is, I can't think of *anybody* who would be doing it. Mark doesn't fit the physical description, and Gary's expression gave away the fact that he didn't know what I was talking about when I mentioned it to him. If it's not one of them, I don't know who it would be."

Zack took a large gulp of his coffee, expressing approval by simply saying, "Dude."

"So, let's think about this seriously for a minute, now that we have the time," Jenny proposed. "The first incident was at the pharmacy, when my mirror was moved. Then, we had our tires slashed here. After that was the smiley face note on the car on Center Street, and then the note on the hotel door. My face had been made public before any of that, so the person probably saw the picture of me, along with the headline stating why I am here."

"Maybe some guy just thinks you're hot," Zack suggested. "Maybe it's got nothing to do with the case. After all, none of the other detectives are being harassed."

"Okay, I have a few things to say to that. First of all, I doubt it. Second, I am not a cop. I think harassing a cop would have much stiffer consequences than stalking an average citizen, so this person might be smart enough to not mess with the people that could get him in the most trouble. But I do agree with your point, to some degree. The person doing it might be unrelated to the case. It might just be that this person is upset that I claim to be a psychic or something."

"You are a psychic."

"I know, but he might not believe that. Maybe my assertion that I can hear from the dead offends him somehow."

"What are the odds that we have two, separate, totally unrelated loonies running around the same town?"

Jenny looked at her husband with half-closed eyes. "In a town this size? Probably pretty high."

"My nephew will be coming to live with us," Zack explained to the employee at the electronics store, "and he's gotten into trouble in the past. I want to be able to keep tabs on him to make sure he's only going where he's supposed to."

Jenny marveled at how smoothly Zack was lying, wondering if she should have been concerned about that.

The middle-aged employee only smiled, appearing to buy the story. "How old is your nephew?"

"Nineteen," Zack said. "Old enough to find big trouble, too young to know better."

"You got that right," the salesman said, leading Zack and Jenny to the automotive section of the store. "How sophisticated are you looking to get? We have basic models, where you have to log in online to track the car, or top-of-the-line models that can text you when the car starts moving."

"I want that one," Jenny said. "The top of the line one."

The sales associate showed them a few models, and the couple focused on one in particular. "Is it possible that we can put this on the car and he won't know it?" Zack asked.

"You can," the employee replied. "Just stick it under the bumper, and he'll never know it's there." He leaned in toward Zack. "But wouldn't it be better if he knew about it? Wouldn't that prevent him from going bad places to begin with?"

"Not with this kid," he replied. "He's smart, so if he knows we're tracking his car, he'll just get his friends to drive him." Zack shook his head. "No, I'd rather be able to confront him when he gets home and say, 'I know you've been here.' It might freak more him out if we always know where he is and he doesn't know how."

The man smiled. "I like the way you think."

Jenny did, too.

Glancing at the dashboard clock as they approached Mark's house, Jenny noted, "It's ten-thirty. Do you think he's still sleeping?"

"I would be, if it were me," Zack replied. "He didn't get home until three in the morning. Even if he went straight to bed, he hasn't gotten eight hours yet. I think a lot of bachelors like at least that much sleep, if not more."

"I hope you're right. The one thing I don't want to have happen is that we're in the middle of putting the tracking device on his car when he comes outside to go somewhere."

"Don't worry. I've got a plan," Zack said.

She glanced at him, wondering what he had in mind. After seeing how smoothly he handled the man in the electronics store, she had confidence that he would pull this off, too.

Jenny's pulse raced as they turned onto Mark's street, seeing the car parked in the same place it had been the night before. "Pull up close to it," Zack instructed. "I mean, so close you are almost kissing his bumper."

She did as she was told, stopping the car when she was mere inches from Mark's.

"Showtime," Zack announced as he got out of the car. He tucked the tracking device under his shirt, walking around and inspecting Mark's bumper. With one hand, he slid the tracking device underneath; with the other, he traced the surface of the bumper, as if to inspect it for damage. Standing up straight and looking around, he gave Jenny a thumbs-up and jogged back to the passenger side. He hopped in the car, shut the door and said to Jenny, "See that? Like a champ."

Jenny left the spot quickly, hoping to do so without being seen—by anybody. Not Mark, and not their stalker. The thought made her shudder.

"Now to go back to the hotel," she said, "pump a long-overdue bottle and get some sleep."

"Yup," Zack replied. "Apparently, until this guy is caught, we're going to be nocturnal."

As tired as she was, sleep was difficult for Jenny. The caffeine she'd used to keep herself awake was doing its job, and it didn't get the memo that it was now nap time. The result was a terrible case of the shakes and a mind that went a hundred miles an hour, despite her body's inability to move due to the fatigue.

With her exhaustion keeping her relaxed, her mind buzzed with snippets of exchanges with Mark. "You look like you've already started," he said, looking at a license.

"Hell, yeah, I've started," a female voice said from within Jenny.

The scene switched. She was walking out of the bar in giant mass of people, glancing over her shoulder, seeing Mark smiling and waving at her. She was leaning on one of her friends to stay upright.

In a new image, she danced her way up to the front door, giving a celebratory shout, handing her license over to the bouncer. "The party can start now. We're here!"

This bouncer wasn't Mark. He was shorter and stockier.

Jenny's eyes popped open as she wondered if one of the girls had just solved her mystery for her. Had Mark recruited one of his coworkers to be his partner in crime? Was this the man that had been harassing her? She closed her eyes again, not moving, trying to remember the details of his face. Once she felt comfortable that she had committed his likeness to memory, she reached for her phone to call Kyle. Hopefully, he'd be able to put a name to that face.

When she looked at her screen, she realized she'd missed a text.

Mark's car was in motion.

Chapter 21

Her heart jumped into her throat, although she quickly realized Mark was not about to strike in the daytime. She blinked repeatedly, trying to get her tired eyes to focus better, eventually getting a clear picture of the map on her screen. The car was currently on a main road and was moving, so he could have been accomplishing any number of things.

With the initial surge of adrenaline leaving her body, she relaxed into the pillow, lowering the phone so she could see it while lying on her side. The screen quickly flipped to become horizontal, which she didn't want. She grunted as she shook it, holding it vertically. The little blue arrow skirting across the screen quickly became hypnotic, and her eyelids became heavy.

She woke with a start, unaware of just how long she'd been sleeping. Silently berating herself, she hoped her moment of carelessness didn't cost a young woman her life. In a panic, she looked at her phone, noticing the blue arrow was now on a side street somewhere. She wished she was more familiar with the area.

Forcing herself to sit up, she watched as the car made a right turn, and then another. It seemed to drive slowly, as if in a residential neighborhood. After another right turn, the car had come full-circle and was passing the same place it had before. "Screen shot," she said out loud, trying to remember what buttons she needed to push to make that happen. Her brain was foggy, her nerves tingled and the importance of this moment was in the forefront of her mind. "Screen shot! How do I do a friggin screen shot?"

All at once, she remembered the procedure, pressing and holding the proper buttons until she heard the click. She breathed a sigh of relief, collapsing her posture a bit, as she continued to watch the car. It repeated similar movements in two other neighborhoods, circling, although Jenny wasn't sure which specific houses he was targeting. She also didn't know how many circles he had made before she woke up. She wanted to kick herself.

The arrow made its way back to Hazel Drive, stopping in a spot similar to where the tracking device had been attached in the first place. Happy to take a break, she set the alarm on her phone for seven o'clock and drifted back off to sleep.

Jenny had texted the images to Zack so they could use his phone to look at the still shots while monitoring Mark's current location from Jenny's phone. For the time being, it appeared he remained at home.

Most of the dinner patrons had left the hotel restaurant, allowing Zack and Jenny alone to freely discuss their plan for the night. "It looks like he circled these three areas," she said, referring to the cartoonish map of the Bennett area that had been available for free at the check-in desk. "When I looked at them on a satellite image, all three places seemed to have small houses lining the streets. He could have been scoping out a hundred different homes."

"We're better off parking near where he lives and just watching him. If we try to hang out by one of those targeted areas, we might choose the wrong one. He works quickly—by the time we catch up with him, he might be done already."

Jenny nodded. "I hope he has to work tonight. Then we'll be able to know where he is for the majority of the evening. As it is now, he could head out at any time, and that's horrifying."

"He could head out soon," Zack said, "but I don't think he's going to attack anybody until much later. These are college kids. They probably go to bed late. He couldn't be guaranteed that they'd be asleep until well after midnight. Probably even later if these girls are partiers."

"This could be another long night," she muttered.

"It'll be worth it if we can catch him."

Just as Jenny was about to agree, she glanced down at her phone and announced. "Time to go. He's on the move."

Mark's car stopped on Seven Springs Road, which was not one of the areas he had circled earlier in the day—at least, not to Jenny's knowledge. He may have scoped that place out while she had still been sleeping.

From the passenger seat of the rental car, Zack looked at Jenny's phone and guided her toward where Mark's vehicle was parked. "Take a right on Harrison Avenue," he instructed, "it should be the third cross street. It looks like a major intersection."

Jenny drove as quickly as she could without putting herself in danger of getting pulled over. While she was on the side of the road getting a speeding ticket, Mark Neighbors could have been slitting the throat of an innocent woman, and she couldn't allow that to happen.

Zack apparently sensed her fear. "I doubt he's attacking anybody right now. It's too early in the night. We should be fine."

Jenny wished she could have shared in his confidence. After taking the right Zack had suggested, she followed his instructions to get to Seven Springs Road. Mark had been at that location for about five minutes total; she wondered if that had been enough time for him to do the unthinkable.

His car was in the driveway of a small ranch house, where lights shone through the bay window of the family room. Beyond the open curtains, she could see two men inside, appearing to watch television—one of them she recognized to be Mark. She continued to drive past the house in order to remain inconspicuous, but the relief that surged through her body almost left her without control of her limbs. She could barely press the gas pedal with her tingling foot.

"I told you," Zack said, "it's too early."

Jenny didn't mind hearing the I-told-you-so. She was just glad he had been right. "Okay," she said in a huge exhale, "we're not too late. We need to just park down the road from him and not let him leave our sight."

"As long as he doesn't leave in a friend's car, we should be all set."

Jenny hated those words. The tracking device could easily have been useless. "We have to be able to see him leave. We can't afford to be sitting here keeping tabs on an empty car while he's out killing somebody. Do me a favor, though...when I drive by again, can you get a look at the house number where he is?"

"That's a can-do."

After circling the block, she passed the house again, trying to be slow enough for Zack to read the number, but not so slow as to attract attention to her car. Zack was able to get the address; whether or not she had been inconspicuous remained to be seen.

"Twenty-five-twenty-one," he said.

"Perfect. Now don't let me forget that before I can call Kyle."

Zack began a twenty-five-twenty-one mantra as they looped around the block. By the time they parked, Zack had repeated it so many times that Jenny didn't think she'd ever be able to forget that number.

A quick press of a button got her on the phone with Kyle. "I really need a favor," she said as soon as he picked up. "I mean, like, now, if possible."

"Sure, what is it?" he asked.

"Can you please tell me who lives at twenty-five-twenty-one Seven Springs Road in Bennett?"

"That should be easy enough," he replied. "Let me get on that. I'll text you the name."

"You're my hero," she said before she hung up.

She bobbed her foot nervously as she waited for his repsonse. Her phone chirped rather quickly, stating, *The house is owned by Tanner and Sophia Kirkland.*

Jenny relayed the information to Zack. "Who is that?" he asked.

"I don't know, but I would assume they are a married couple. I doubt he's in there attacking the wife, especially considering he looked like he was just casually hanging out with that other guy.

"So, these are just friends of Mark's?"

"That's what I'm guessing. Let me check something out, though." She shot a text back to Kyle. *Can I have pictures of them, please?*

The response came almost immediately. *That will take a little more time. Hang on.*

The couple sat wordlessly as they waited. Zack reached down and pulled the lever next to his seat, causing the back to recline. Jenny leaned her elbow against the window sill, using her hand to hold her head up. After a while, a chirp caused Jenny to look at her phone, which had a picture of a woman on the screen. She appeared to be an Italian woman with dark hair and eyes, looking to be in her mid-to-late twenties. This woman didn't seem familiar to Jenny in any capacity; it seemed that neither she nor the victims had ever come into contact with her. Soon, another photo appeared, scooting Sophia's picture out of the way.

It was the stocky bouncer she had seen in her vision earlier in the day.

"Uh oh," Jenny said. "This might be trouble."

"Why? What's up?"

"The guy who lives here works with Mark at Shenanigans. But it isn't his job that scares me, it's his build."

"Ah," Zack said. "I'm guessing he's stocky and he might be our note-writing friend?"

"Yes," Jenny replied, "those friendly little notes. Do you think they're in there conspiring as we speak?"

"It looked more like they were watching a baseball game, if you ask me."

Letting out a sigh, Jenny said, "I certainly hope you are right."

Jenny's bottom felt numb. She had already peed in somebody's front yard, and she was feeling the urge to do it again. The past few hours of surveillance had felt like days. "I think he's having a sleepover," she said with a yawn.

"This stake-out business isn't all it's cracked up to be. You'd think that being a cop or a private investigator would be cool, but if this is what it's like, it's not really all that fun."

"I'm sure Kyle would tell you it's not always a laugh a minute."

Silence took over the car again. Zack stretched. Jenny took a mint out of her purse and popped it in her mouth. They waited.

And they waited some more.

Eventually, Jenny noticed some tail lights in what appeared to be the driveway where Mark had parked. "Zack," she said with a nudge, "this might be it."

They both sat up straighter as Jenny grasped the key and Zack turned on the phone. The car backed out of the driveway, heading in Zack and Jenny's direction. She muttered a few choice swear words under her breath as he passed them, but he didn't seem to recognize their car or notice that there were people sitting inside it.

"That's him," Zack said. "At least, that's his car." He held up the phone. "We have movement."

Waiting until the monitored vehicle was safely around the corner and out of sight, Jenny turned the key and maneuvered a three-point turn. Soon, she was following in the path outlined by the blue arrow.

A quick glance at the clock showed it was three-fifteen.

"I'm not sure what outcome I'm hoping for," Jenny said nervously. "Part of me hopes he just goes home to bed, but we'll never catch him that way."

"It doesn't matter what we hope for," Zack replied. "We're going to get what we get. He just turned left."

"Onto what street?"

Zack squinted at the screen. "Looks like Elwood Avenue."

Jenny read the street signs until Elwood Avenue came into sight. Taking a left, she didn't see tail lights in front of her.

"Right on Cooperstown," Zack added.

Putting on her high-beams, Jenny looked for the street sign, feeling relief when she found it. They proceeded this way for several minutes until Zack announced, "His car just stopped."

"Where?" Jenny asked.

"Talmadge Road," he replied. "One of the places he circled this afternoon."

Chapter 22

"Oh my God, you're kidding," Jenny said.

"I wish I was," Zack assured her.

"Where do I go?"

"Left on Spruce, then another left on Talmadge."

"Oh my God. Oh my God. Oh my God." Jenny kept the chant going in a whisper as her whole body tensed. If she missed a turn, someone could literally die. The sign for Spruce appeared, and she made the left.

"Talmadge shouldn't be that far," Zack said.

His words turned out to be true. She took a left again, gunning the gas pedal, unsure how far down the road she needed to go. After about thirty seconds, Mark's car appeared, parked along the right side of the road.

Now to figure out which house he was targeting.

As soon as their car ground to a halt, Zack was outside looking around. Jenny joined him soon after, hearing Zack say, "There he is."

She followed the direction of Zack's pointed finger, seeing only a shadow hop down from a side window and disappear into the backyard of the house.

Zack started to run in that direction, but Jenny shouted, "Zack, don't! He has a knife!" She dialed the police.

Instead of following Mark, Zack ran to the front door of the house, ringing the bell incessantly.

"Nine-one-one, what is your emergency?"

"We need the police to come out to Talmadge Road. Now. We just caught a man trying to break into a woman's window."

"What's the house number?"

Jenny looked at the mailbox. "Eighty-six-oh-three."

"Where is the man now?"

The porch light of the house came on, and Jenny could see more light peek out from behind the curtain, which the person inside had just moved out of place to see what was going on.

"He ran into the backyard," Jenny explained. "He's wearing dark clothes. We can't see him anymore. I think his name is Mark Neighbors."

"Please!" Zack shouted to the person inside as he knocked feverishly. "Open the door! We just caught someone trying to break into your house!"

It worried Jenny that she didn't know where Mark was. He could have been breaking into someone else's house for all she knew. A thought popped into her head. She reached in the car and pressed the horn, not releasing it for several seconds.

She did it again.

Lights came on all around her. The neighbors were most likely upset, but they were awake—and they wouldn't be attacked in their sleep by Mark Neighbors.

"Police have been dispatched," the operator said. "What's happening now?"

"I'm waking the neighbors," Jenny replied, wailing on the horn again. "I don't want anyone to be caught off guard if he tries to break into someone else's house."

"What the hell's the matter with you?" a man's voice called. She saw his silhouette on his front porch.

The front door of the victimized house opened, and a young woman stood in the entryway. Jenny couldn't hear what Zack was saying to her above the horn, but she could see the woman put her hand over her mouth and step outside. Zack led her to the side of the house where Mark had been, pointing at the window.

"Shut up!" somebody screamed.

"They hate me now," Jenny muttered, "but they will love me in the morning."

"Can you see the intruder now?" the operator asked.

"No, ma'am," Jenny said, "I still can't. And that terrifies me."

Jenny heard the operator speak, although she knew it wasn't to her. "We'll need the canine unit to track the suspect. He may have gone into hiding."

The canine unit. Jenny smiled. The dogs would find him, no doubt.

"Oh my God, lay off the horn!" someone else yelled.

Feeling as if the entire neighborhood had already been woken up, Jenny did just that.

Without the sound of the horn, she could make out the sirens in the distance. "I hear them," Jenny said. "The police are on their way."

"Stay on the phone with me until they get there, okay?"

"Yes, ma'am."

It seemed to take forever for the police to arrive. The sirens kept getting louder, but she must have originally heard them from miles away. Finally, red and blue lights rounded the corner, eventually coming so close that their brightness was blinding. She shielded her eyes as the officers rushed out of the car.

"He went that way," Jenny told them, pointing behind the woman's house. "He was trying to break into a window on the side of the house."

The brave officers trotted off into the darkness, hands on their weapons. She hoped they didn't get ambushed.

"They're here," she told the operator over the phone. "Thanks for your help." She hung up as several more police cars arrived. Most of the officers scattered to find Mark, but a few stayed behind.

One male officer approached Jenny. "Are you the one who called?"

"Yes, sir."

He held his flashlight above his shoulder, fixating it on Jenny. "Hey," he said, "I know you. You're the psychic."

"Exactly," Jenny said, "and this guy is the serial killer you've been looking for all along." She gestured over her shoulder with her thumb. "Not Gary Kimbrough."

He paused for a moment, apparently unsure what to say. "What happened here?"

"He was trying to break into a window." Releasing a sigh, she added, "Rachel Moore let me know in a vision that Mark Neighbors was her killer. My husband and I put a tracking device on his car, so we know he'd circled this house a few times earlier today. Sure enough, he came back out here tonight, but we were following him. When we pulled up just a few minutes ago, he was trying to get into the window. He left when he heard my husband say we'd found him."

"And which direction did he go?"

Jenny pointed. "Around the house. That way."

"That his car?" The officer aimed his flashlight at Mark's vehicle.

"Sure is."

Another squad car pulled up, and Jenny saw the outline of a man emerge, led by an overly-excited German Shepard.

"Grandy. Over here," the officer who was speaking with Jenny said.

The canine patrol officer walked over with the dog, who looked like it was about to have the time of its life. "What's the scenario?"

"The guy was caught breaking into a window, and then he ran off behind the house. That's the perp's car. I bet you can get a scent off that."

"Excellent," the canine officer said. "Come on, Lexi."

The dog trotted off and was led to the driver's side door of Mark's car. With a single gesture, the officer commanded the dog to sniff the handle. Lexi's tail wagged as she took in the scent.

"Okay, Lexi," he said firmly, "find it."

The dog ran excitedly in a back and forth pattern, nose to the ground, heading straight for the window that Mark had just tried to climb into. Jenny watched as Lexi paused there for a moment, circling around, before leading her handler right along the path Mark had taken into the darkness.

"He can run, but he can't hide," Jenny remarked with a smile.

"Nope," the officer replied. "Lexi will find him. She always does."

At that moment, Zack approached with his arm around the woman who lived in the house. Jenny couldn't imagine the fear and confusion going on in that poor woman's head. One minute she had been sound asleep; the next moment she was waking up to a nightmare.

"Are you the resident?" the officer asked the shaken woman.

She nodded wearily. "Yeah, I live here."

"Can you tell me what happened?"

Looking bewildered, she replied, "I don't even know. I woke up when I heard my doorbell ringing. Apparently, somebody was trying to break into my window?" Tucking her hair behind her ear, she added, "I thought they caught that guy."

Jenny closed her eyes, trying to swallow her anger toward Gary Kimbrough. Now that she was actually able to lay eyes on the woman whose life was put into jeopardy because of his false confession, her hate toward the man multiplied. Maintaining her self-control, however, she simply said, "Sadly, I think they arrested the wrong man."

The officer didn't argue.

"Tell me," Jenny asked the woman, "do you ever go to Shenanigans?"

"Yeah, I do," the victim said.

Jenny looked at the policeman. "And there's your connection."

The sound of aggressive barking interrupted the conversation. They all looked in the direction of the noise, hearing an officer shout, "Come out with your hands up!"

Lexi snarled and growled like she wanted to tear Mark apart; the sick and twisted part of Jenny wished they would let her.

"Get on the ground! Hands behind your back!"

While she couldn't see any of the action, those were the best words Jenny could have ever heard. It was over. The women of Bennett were once again safe, and she could go back to her baby. The thought of it made her feel physically lighter.

Out of the darkness, three officers walked with their hands on Mark, who was cuffed and hanging his head. They were heading to one of the patrol cars when Jenny asked the officer, "Can I go over and spit on him?"

"Nah," he replied, sounding amused. "Your DNA might mess with the evidence. Let his fellow inmates take care of him; they'll make sure justice is served."

She knew of the hierarchy that existed inside prison walls; she wondered how low Mark would be on it.

Her thoughts were interrupted by the sight of officers unraveling a large roll of crime scene tape around the entire property. She had to step out of the way so that she would end up on the civilian side of it.

"Jenny," she heard a familiar voice say. She turned around to see a silhouette of a man approaching her. Although she couldn't see his face until he got right up next to her, she knew it was Chief DePalo from his voice. "Clearly, I owe you an apology," he announced, "and a huge thank you."

"It's no problem, sir," Jenny replied. "I'm just glad it all worked out."

He shook his head. "I should have had more faith in you."

"Under the circumstances, I can see why you didn't. To be honest, I still have no idea how Gary Kimbrough knew details of the crime scene that he shouldn't have."

"Loose lips," the chief said. "Just a few hours ago, we figured out that one of our rookie officers had told the details to his wife, who told her sister, who told her neighbor—who happened to be Gary's aunt. He overheard the conversation."

"Oh, dear," Jenny said.

"Yeah, we're going to have a little chat with Rookie when this is all over."

She watched the officers lead Mark to the car, opening the back door and pushing his head down as they guided him inside. The door closed behind him.

"Well, I just wanted to come over and thank you, but now I've got a lot to take care of," Chief DePalo said as he put his hand on Jenny's shoulder.

"By all means. But before you go, I want to give you one more name."

"And who is that?"

"Tanner Kirkland," Jenny replied. "Something tells me he's in on this, and he's the guy who has been harassing me."

"Tanner Kirkland," the chief repeated, "got it." He smiled and walked away.

Chapter 23

Jenny sat the car seat down in the foyer of Mick and John's townhouse. As Lucy, the dog, curiously sniffed Steve from head to toe, Jenny greeted Mick with what she reminded herself was just a friendly hug. "Wow, he's gotten big," Mick noted, looking at the baby.

"Tell me about it," Jenny said. "He's growing so fast." She picked the car seat up again as they walked into the living room. "It looks great," she added, looking around. "I love what you've done with the place."

Mick laughed, his beautiful blue eyes twinkling. "We just added a few comforts of home, that's all."

"Well, it looks nice. So, how are things going?" Jenny took the baby out of his car seat and held him—something she hadn't been able to stop doing ever since she'd gotten home from Missouri the day before.

"They're going well," Mick said, inviting Jenny to sit down on the couch.

She took a seat, placing little Steve on her lap. "Really?" she said skeptically. "The reason I wanted to come here a little early was so you could tell me the truth."

"I am telling the truth, I promise." He chose the recliner across the room. "John was recommended for outpatient treatment, and he goes faithfully without argument."

Jenny looked at him sternly for a moment before breaking into a smile. "Good," she said, "I'm glad to hear it."

An adorable, petite woman came down the stairs, gasping when she saw the baby in Jenny's lap. This must have been Mick's girlfriend—the woman Jenny approved of, in theory, but was jealous of nonetheless.

"Oh my goodness, your baby is so cute," she gushed.

"You can hold him, if you'd like."

"Really?" Her face grew even more endearing than it had been before. She held out her hands, wriggling her fingers, eagerly approaching Steve. After carefully taking him from Jenny, she hugged him tightly into her body, sniffing his scent. Jenny could see—and feel—the love pouring out of this woman, who let out a sound that could only be described as a squeal. "Mick…couldn't you just eat him up?"

Mick laughed again, replying, "I agree he's cute, but I don't know about *eating* him."

"Oh, you're no fun," the woman said. "I'm Samantha, by the way."

Even her name was cute.

"Hi, I'm Jenny."

"I've heard all about you, and I can't thank you enough. You've helped both Mick and my brother." Settling the baby on one of her hips, she placed her free hand on her heart. "I mean it. I feel like I owe you so much."

"Well, just make sure this guy doesn't drink and we'll be even." She gestured to Mick with her thumb. "Oh, and treat him well, too. There's that."

Samantha and Mick exchanged a loving glance. "No worries there," she assured Jenny.

Oh, dear.

The front door opened, and in walked John. He greeted everyone with a smile, looking back and forth between Samantha and Mick. "Is there something you guys haven't told me?"

"What, that I've spontaneously given birth to a four-month-old?" Samantha asked.

"Just kidding," John assured her. He walked over to Jenny, who stood when he approached. While hugging her, he said, "It's good to see you."

"I'm so glad to hear you say that," she said genuinely. "I thought you might hate me." Releasing the embrace, she added, "Mick, here, has told me that you're doing well."

Smiling sheepishly, he said, "Yeah, I'm okay...now. I'm not exactly proud of the way I acted before, though."

Jenny shooed away the comment with her hand. "Don't worry about that. We ambushed you, and you reacted the way anybody would have under those circumstances. It's no big deal."

Still looking embarrassed, he said, "Treatment is going well, though. I have to go in for meetings every other day. It helps—I am in sessions with other people who are in my stage of the game. Most of them have relapsed a time or two, and it's good to know that it's normal."

"I'm sure it is," Jenny said. "If drugs were easy to kick, there wouldn't be any treatment facilities."

"It's the hardest thing I've ever done in my life."

The topic of conversation went to their work with the Wounded Warrior Project. They told stories about making house modifications for people who came home from the war with disabilities, lining up contractors and making sure the work was done properly. Both men commented on how rewarding the work was and that it gave them a reason to stay clean.

After a while, Jenny took the baby, who was now sleeping, out of Samantha's arms and put him back in his car seat. A short drive later, she was back at the house, still feeling exhausted from her schedule-altering trip to Missouri. She managed to stay awake until the baby went to sleep for the evening, but she hit the sheets right after he did at seven-thirty.

Her sleep was sound until the middle of the night, when she heard Baxter barking softly under his breath. The sound was little more than a muffled *oof*.

"Bax, shhh."

She had just about dozed off again when he let out another subdued woof.

"Oh, God, are you serious?" she muttered, rolling over onto her back.

The process repeated enough times for Jenny to become wide awake and aware of the fact that she was hungry. "Seriously, dog," she whispered as her feet hit the floor, "if I didn't need to eat, you'd be out on your ear."

She shuffled groggily toward the kitchen, working her way through the dark hallway, Baxter at her feet. The dog ran ahead of her, his chain jingling as he went into the living room.

She turned the kitchen light on, but something didn't seem right. The dog's chain continued to jingle from the other room. Peeking around the doorway, she saw Baxter eagerly receiving love from a man she immediately recognized to be Leo Pryzbyck.

Leo Pryzbyck, the man who had brutally killed a woman back in the eighties but remained free due to the neighbor's wrongful conviction.

Leo Pryzbyck, the man who had threatened both Jenny and her then-unborn baby when she figured out he had been the actual killer.

Leo Pryzbyck, the man who had left town before the authorities could catch him.

Leo Pryzbyck.

She let out a gasp and a shriek at the same time, covering her mouth with both hands. The last thing she wanted to do was wake anyone else in the house and put them in danger. Leo was a violent man—he had killed before—and Jenny had made the police aware of that. He had managed to leave town before the police could catch him, and he'd been on the run ever since.

And now he was in her living room with a gun in his hand.

"Jenny Larrabee," he said softly. "We meet again." His free hand continued to scratch Baxter's head.

Frozen with fear, she simply looked at him, saying nothing.

"It was so nice to see you in my neck of the woods the past few days. I even left you some nice little notes. Did you get them?" His voice had a friendly quality to it, which made him that much more frightening.

Jenny remained silent.

"It was a shame you left so quickly," he went on, taking a few steps toward her. "We didn't have the chance to meet in person."

She backed up, returning to the kitchen. He followed her, stepping into the brightness, looking just as haggard as she had remembered. The one quality she hadn't noticed before was his stockiness, but that was painfully obvious to her now.

"Where are you going, Jenny? Do you think you can outrun me?" He walked a little closer. With a smile, he added, "In case you haven't noticed, there's nowhere for you to run."

Her mind immediately went to her baby, wondering if he had been in the house long enough to do something horrible to Steve. She didn't know what to do—she would have been willing to stand there and take a bullet if it meant he'd leave the baby alone...but what if he had already hurt him? Or what if he killed Jenny and then went to the baby's room and did something awful afterward? If only she knew what she could do to keep her son safe, she would have been willing to do it, no matter what it was.

A loud sound permeated the room, causing Jenny to jump three feet in the air. It was only Baxter, barking at the pantry, looking for a treat. She closed her eyes and sucked in a shaky breath, taking a moment to realize that sound hadn't been a gunshot and she was, for the time being, very much alive.

The dog barked again. "Bax, hush!" she commanded. *Please do not wake everyone up*, she silently implored. If they didn't come out of bed, perhaps they'd survive this.

Even if she didn't.

"That's a cute dog you have there," Leo said softly. "I've always wanted a dog."

Don't hurt Baxter. She thought it but didn't say it, fearful that her worlds would have backfired if she said them out loud.

"Maybe I'll take him with me back to Bennett..." Leo's eyes looked crazed as they focused on Jenny. "You know, that place where—thanks to you—*I can't even use my own name.*" He took another step closer, now only a few feet from Jenny. "Everything had been fine in my life, you know that? Nobody had mentioned Stella's name in *years*." He spoke through gritted teeth, his hate for Jenny palpable. "And you had to go and *fuck everything up.* My life is *ruined* now. Do you understand that? It's *ruined!*"

Jenny's eyes flitted back and forth between Leo's face and his gun, which, for the time being, was still by his side. She hoped he would come just a little bit closer—within striking distance. If she was going to be killed in this kitchen, fine, but she wasn't going down without a fight.

"How is killing me going to make anything better?" she asked. "It would only make matters worse for you. Then you'd be faced with two counts of murder."

He smiled, sending a chill down Jenny's spine. "Not if people don't know it was me. Why would they suspect *Michael Smith* from Bennett, Missouri in the shooting death of a woman in Tennessee? I'm sure you've messed with enough people's lives that there are a whole *slew* of people who want to kill you. Besides...they haven't been able to find me yet, and I doubt they'll find me now."

"Don't you have a car parked outside? Somebody might have seen it."

"Yeah, I do." He smiled before adding, "A stolen one."

Jenny wanted to keep him talking, hoping he would move in closer. "You never answered my question. How will killing me make it better?"

Edging just a tiny bit closer, he muttered, "I have done nothing but think about you and what you've done to me since the day I left Ed's house. You took my life from me. And now I want to take your life from..."

BAM!

The sound was deafening, and Leo suddenly fell to the ground. She looked at him in shock as he lay on her floor, motionless and bleeding. Glancing up, she saw her mother in her nightgown with one hand holding a gun and the other covering her mouth.

"Ma!" Jenny exclaimed in surprise.

"Is he dead?" Isabelle asked with fear. "Did I kill him?"

Jenny couldn't answer. She didn't even care to check. Stepping over Leo on the floor, she ran down the hall into the baby's room, turning on the light and rushing to the crib. Steve lay still on his back, arms overhead. He was a beautiful pink color, but to be sure, Jenny put her hand in front of his mouth, where she felt the subtle, warm hint of baby breath. Her knees immediately buckled, and she collapsed to the floor with relief.

Zack rounded the corner of the bedroom. "Jenny, what the hell happened?"

She lowered herself to her back, lying on the floor, tears streaming from her eyes. "The baby's fine. Go check on my mom."

"Are you hurt?" he demanded.

"No. Go to the kitchen. My mom shot Leo Pryzbyck."

"What?" After a pause from apparent confusion, Zack disappeared from the doorway. Jenny knew that she, too, needed to go check on her mother, but for the moment she couldn't get up. The thought that she may have just lost her baby was too much for her to bear, leaving her without an ounce of strength in her body.

Breathing deeply a few times, she managed to flip over onto her hands and knees, willing herself into a standing position. Her steps were wobbly as she went back out to the kitchen, seeing her mother seated on a chair, pale as a ghost, with the gun on the table. Zack was on the phone, giving the address.

She looked at Leo, who remained in the same position on the floor. His eyes were open, but glossy. His stare was blank. "Is he alive?" Jenny asked her mother.

Robotically, Isabelle replied, "I don't think so. Is the baby okay?"

Jenny walked over to her mother, standing behind her chair, bending over and wrapping her arms around Isabelle's neck. "Yes, the baby's fine. You saved us, Mom," she whispered. "All of us."

Isabelle reached up her hand, placing it on Jenny's arm. She patted it a few times, but didn't say anything.

"How did you know?" Jenny asked.

"I heard the dog bark." Her voice was distant. "I'd never heard Baxter bark in the middle of the night, so I thought something might have been going on. I came upstairs and saw him cornering you. I couldn't have that."

Jenny sympathized with her mother. The thought of losing a baby was horrifying, no matter what age the child was.

Zack's voice became clear to Jenny. "No, he doesn't appear to be," he told the dispatcher. "He's not moving."

"I just killed a man," Isabelle whispered. "Somebody's son."

"It was him or me," Jenny assured her. "He'd killed before; I'm sure he would have done it again."

Isabelle released a breath, her cheeks puffing out with the force. "I don't know if I can live with this."

"You did the right thing. I'm positive he would have killed me, and then I don't know what he would have done with Steve." She shuddered at the thought. "You're a hero, Ma."

"The baby's really okay?"

With a smile gracing her lips for the first time since this all began, Jenny said, "He didn't even wake up."

Zack lowered the phone from his mouth, speaking over it to Jenny and Isabelle. "Can you two wait by the front door for the cops to come? I'll stay here and guard him." He gestured his head toward Leo.

"You okay to get up, Ma?" Jenny asked.

She nodded, although she accepted Jenny's offer to help her get out of the chair. "I'd rather not look at him anymore, anyway."

Leading her mother toward the front door, Jenny asked, "When, exactly, did you get a gun?"

"Back when I told you that you should get one and you didn't."

Jenny smiled. "How did you learn how to shoot it?"

"I go to target practice every Tuesday." When Jenny only responded with a laugh, Isabelle added, "What? Do you think I sit down there all day and do nothing?"

Six weeks later

"Jenny? Are you ready?" Isabelle knocked on the door to the upstairs as she opened it.

"Almost," Jenny replied, putting the finishing touches on a diaper change, which wasn't easy since Steve spent the whole time trying to roll over. She grabbed his leg and flipped him onto his back—again—and said, "Stay still, squiggly butt."

Once the diaper was on and the handoff to Zack was complete, both women grabbed their guns, walked out the door and headed for the shooting range.

To be continued in Cold...

Made in the USA
Coppell, TX
18 February 2025